Cm

WHEN THEY HEADED FOR GILA BEND, THEY HEADED FOR TROUBLE . . .

Rado Kane—the infamous gunfighter hired to end a feud between two families in Gila Bend. Pitted against the ruthless Jack Sandeen, Rado knows the price of peace will be blood—and lots of it.

Miss Crystal Richmond—a beautiful brunette with theatrical aspirations. This trip could be her ticket to stardom . . . or an untimely death.

Reverend Gideon Cull—his mission is more than delivering the Lord's message—ask any of the wealthy widows who trusted him, only to discover too late that his intentions were less than saintly.

Juan Carlos Santiago Morales—as leader of the Mexican banditos, he spills blood with no mercy . . . until his price is met.

Jack Sandeen—the cold-blooded gunfighter who kills for business *and* pleasure. Now, he'd like nothing more than to blast Rado Kane to hell.

The Stagecoach Series
Ask your bookseller for the books you have missed

STAGECOACH STATION 49:

GILA BEND

Hank Mitchum

Created by the producers of
The Holts: An American Dynasty,
The Badge, and **White Indian.**

Book Creations, Inc., Canaan, NY • Lyle Kenyon Engle, Founder

BANTAM BOOKS
NEW YORK • TORONTO • LONDON • SYDNEY • AUCKLAND

GILA BEND

*A Bantam Book / published by arrangement with
Book Creations, Inc.*

Bantam edition / September 1990

*Produced by Book Creations, Inc.
Lyle Kenyon Engel, Founder*

ISBN 0-553-28604-8

Published simultaneously in the United States and Canada

*Bantam Books are published by Bantam Books, a division of Bantam
Doubleday Dell Publishing Group, Inc. Its trademark, consisting of
the words "Bantam Books" and the portrayal of a rooster, is
Registered in U.S. Patent and Trademark Office and in other
countries. Marca Registrada. Bantam Books, 666 Fifth Avenue,
New York, New York 10103.*

PRINTED IN THE UNITED STATES OF AMERICA

RAD   0 9 8 7 6 5 4 3 2 1

STAGECOACH STATION 49:

GILA BEND

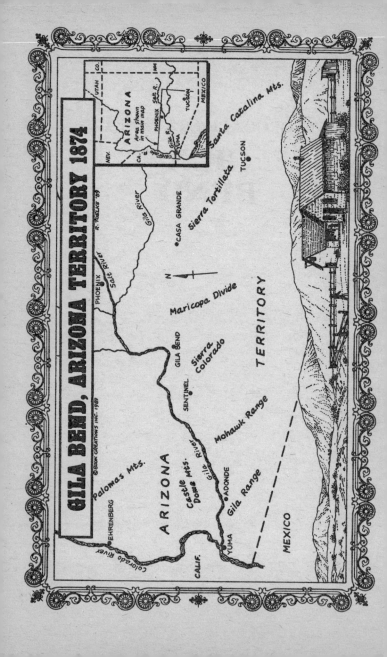

Chapter One

Sam Loomis pulled himself up onto the driver's box of the red Concord stagecoach and settled down on the right side of the seat. He pushed back his hat, revealing his graying brown hair, and pulled out his pocket watch. It was 7:45 A.M.—fifteen minutes to departure if they were to be on schedule, and knowing the driver, Loomis knew he would insist on being on schedule whether the passengers were ready or not, because Walt Grader was a man of exact habit. So was Sam Loomis, for that matter, and his every action as shotgun guard was part of the careful routine he had perfected over the four years he had been on that particular run.

Squinting briefly at the sun breaking over the eastern end of Yuma was part of that routine, as was the same narrowed gaze he gave his immediate surroundings. It was a long and slow look, beginning at the back of the stage, where he briefly saw the Concord clerks loading the mail sacks and passenger luggage into the rear boot of the coach. From there his glance swung slowly back around to the front of the vehicle and to the six well-groomed horses that were in the final stages of being hitched.

Loomis's blue eyes paused only for a moment as he gave his customary nod to the two handlers doing the hitching. Then he completed the circuit, stopping for precisely three heartbeats to stare into the eyes of each person in the arc of his turn—any eyes that were looking at

1

him, that is. And it usually happened that most were, because Sam Loomis was a very impressive figure.

He stood six feet three and weighed two hundred twenty pounds, every ounce of which seemed to be carefully applied to his thick-bodied, hard-muscled frame. At age fifty-two in that autumn of 1874, he was harder and tougher than most men half his age, and he knew it. Just about anyone assessing Sam Loomis knew it, too—which made his job a whole lot easier.

The other thing that made the shotgun guard's job easier was Walt Grader. Loomis looked at the driver as he watched the men hitching the team and smiled to himself. Shorter than his co-worker and about ten years younger, Grader was one of the best—at least Loomis figured him to be, and he had sat by the side of a good many drivers. Grader had an air of quiet authority about him, and he carried himself and spoke as a person who would have full command of the stagecoach and its team at all times.

Unlike other drivers the shotgunner had worked with, Grader was quiet, and while he drank as much as the next man, Loomis had never seen him become rowdy or get into a fight. He recalled a time in a Yuma saloon, though, when two men tried to take the driver's measure. Grader had done little more than tell them he was ready when they were—and just the way he had said it immediately caused the challengers to find something urgent that they needed to do in another saloon.

Taking his gaze from Grader, Sam Loomis looked around. This morning there were few people about. Aside from the stage-line employees busily doing their jobs with little talk among themselves, there were the four passengers, all of them waiting on the covered porch to his immediate left. There was also the youth in the alleyway to Loomis's right.

Nineteen years old, hatless, with a lock of black hair covering his forehead and hanging into his brown eyes, the skinny lad was leaning his left shoulder against the building wall as if he just happened to be pausing in a

casual walk around town on a fine morning. But the Colt
.45 revolver he wore in a well-oiled, low-slung holster
thonged to his right thigh said otherwise.

Sam Loomis looked at Billy Nathan for an extra three
heartbeats. He knew something about this particular young
man, and his being up that early in the morning did not
seem natural. It also spelled possible trouble. But Loomis
pulled his mind from the onlooker, for he had the rest of
his routine to complete.

Reaching down to the canvas bag at his feet, his hand
hovered briefly over the four rifles that rested barrel up
beside the bag against the front boot railing. But he ignored the long-barreled Henry and three shorter Win-
chesters for the moment and opened the bag, extracting a
Model 1861 Colt Navy revolver.

He very slowly broke open the weapon and checked
its load before holding the pistol up toward the sky so he
could look through the barrel. Snapping the pistol closed,
he then spun the cylinder, and with a satisfied nod he put
the weapon back into the bag. There were two other
pistols in the bag, and each one was withdrawn and sub-
jected to the same careful, unhurried examination.

Loomis next turned his attention to the Henry rifle
and checked its load and action. Then, again with a determined, slow movement, he nested the butt against his
shoulder and sighted along the rifle's long barrel as he
rotated it ninety degrees.

Loomis paused for a split second with the gunsight
aimed at the boy still standing in the alleyway, and then
he carefully set the Henry alongside the three Winches-
ters resting on the floor of the boot. His show of weaponry
was to demonstrate to anybody watching the folly of attacking this particular stage, and with that in mind, and
wanting any observer to be aware of one other weapon,
the guard reached down behind the canvas bag for his
short-barreled shotgun.

Sawed off on both ends, the two-shot dealer of may-
hem was Loomis's favorite weapon. The gun, after all,

gave him his unofficial job title, for although "security messenger" was what the stage line officially called him, "shotgun guard" was the term that gave him the respect of travelers and townsmen alike. It did not matter to Loomis that the weapon was meant for use in rockier terrain, where a surprise attack was more possible than here in the flats of Arizona Territory. Never mind that in the open desert the far-shooting Henry with its sixteen rounds was the superior weapon. The fact was that the short, thick weapon was taken very seriously by anybody near its business end—and Loomis identified with the gun as a thing of power.

A smile split his weathered face as he put the shotgun back into its place, and the smile, while genuine, was also part of the routine, as he relaxed and surveyed the awaiting passengers. They consisted of two men and two women, an older one and a younger one of each, and they struck Sam Loomis as an interesting foursome.

The older woman was a strange one. Extremely thin, she looked to be somewhere in her sixties with her wrinkled face, but she did not dress her age. As Loomis thought about it, he realized she did not dress as *any* age would, for her clothes were both very flamboyant and oddly put together. Her full skirt was bright red with yellow and orange flowers, and tucked into it was a faded blue denim work shirt. Over the shirt she wore a loosely fitting man's suit jacket, which was a dark shade of brown, while pushed back on her head over snowy white, closely cropped hair was a wide-brimmed straw hat. The purple and blue scarf that was tied around the crown hung down her back almost to her waist.

She looked like the well-used paint board of an artist Loomis had carried on his stage once. A palette, the man had called it, and it had had gobs of hard-dried paint of every color in the rainbow and then some. *Yep*, Sam Loomis thought to himself, *a living, breathing palette. That's what Mrs. Isabel Hallan looks like.* He recalled reading her name on the passenger list. *No doubt a widow woman, and also no doubt that Mr. Hallan had had himself an interesting life with her,* thought Loomis, for certainly he had never seen the likes of her before.

He had also never seen anybody doing what she was doing. Standing on the porch with her back against the station building, she was holding in both her hands a piece of wire that was bent so that it formed a large loop in the middle, much like a handwritten letter *l.* She was twirling the wire slowly so that the loop went round and round, though she was not looking at it at all; rather, she was looking at everything around her, including the stage and the horses, the other passengers, the alleyway, and the boy with the gun—and Sam Loomis.

He shrugged off the strange feeling that suddenly coursed through his body. After all, his whole morning routine was *supposed* to be looked at, was it not? He turned his attention to the younger woman.

Now, she was something to look at, all right. In her mid-twenties, she was thin in all the right places—though perhaps a mite too thin in the other places, but not by much. Her long straight black hair bordered a face that was more than just pretty—or would have been if she were more relaxed—and her hazel eyes seemed slightly troubled. Miss Crystal Richmond, the passenger list said, and the name fit, for she seemed delicate like crystal but at the same time strong. *And,* Loomis mused, *expensive.*

In his experience only three types of women looked as Crystal Richmond did: the wife of somebody rich, the daughter of somebody rich, or the exclusive whore of somebody rich. She wore no wedding ring, so that eliminated the first possibility. But she was an admirable-looking young thing, all right, and in the ensemble she wore—a nip-waisted purple corduroy jacket with a frilly lace jabot spilling over the neckline and a long, slightly bustled skirt—she looked almost like royalty. And like royalty she appeared out of place standing there, as if she should rightfully be elsewhere. Her mind seemed to be somewhere else, too, for she nodded absently when the liquor peddler tried to make some conversation with her, barely noticing his existence.

His name was Lyman Whisters, and he had ridden in Loomis's coaches three times before, all in the past year. From the gray in Whisters's sandy-colored hair and mustache the shotgunner judged him to be about the same age as he himself was. Whisters was also close to Loomis's weight, but the salesman was about half a foot shorter and looked to be a lot softer. His brown-checked suit was in need of a pressing, and his dark brown derby had seen better days, but the man looked generally at peace with himself on this Yuma morning . . . at least now that he was satisfied his cases of liquor were correctly and safely stowed in the rear boot of the coach.

Loomis figured the fourth passenger was anywhere from his late twenties to his mid-thirties, and judging from the way the man's denim jacket and pants fit him, he was about six feet tall and under a hundred eighty pounds. Lean and hard, the man was listed as Mr. Smith. The shotgun guard nodded to himself, thinking that there were lots of Mr. Smiths in the world, which was why most of them insisted on having their first names listed—but not this one.

Unlike the other passengers, this man looked completely at ease, not seeming to have a care in the world—unless it was making sure the battered wooden rocking chair he sat in maintained its slow back-and-forth movement. His boot heels were propped on the porch rail, and his hands were clasped in front of him just below the buckle of his gun belt. His dusty black plainsman's hat was pulled down, covering his eyes, his thick brown hair, and most of his stubbly face. It was evident that he was a man who knew how to relax when he had the chance.

Mr. Smith. Smiling to himself, Sam Loomis decided that he might just possibly be the most interesting of all the passengers that bright morning.

And then his thoughts were interrupted.

*   *   *

After retying the rawhide thong at the bottom of his holster, lashing it tighter around his thigh, Billy Nathan tested his pistol's loose fit. The gun was one of the new Colt models that was short-barreled and meant for fast drawing. He'd only had the gun for a month, and a day had not gone by that he hadn't spent hours practicing his draw, using bottles and cans as targets. This morning, exactly one week after his nineteenth birthday, he would find out if the practice had been worth all the effort, for today's shoot was not to be with bottles or cans—it was to be the real thing.

Pushing back his black hair from his eyes and forehead, Billy Nathan stepped from between the buildings and into the street. As he passed the horses, he looked briefly at the big man up on the stage box. The man was looking at him. *Good,* the youth thought to himself, *another witness to tell the story when my business is finished.*

The old woman in the crazy clothes was watching him, too. She had been looking at him—staring at him, in fact—as she twirled that bent piece of wire. *Well, stare all you want, old lady, 'cause today you'll see somethin' you can tell to all the other old biddies in Tucson or wherever the hell it is you're going!* he proclaimed to himself.

He then glanced at the younger woman waiting on the porch. He had been looking at her earlier, but when she had noticed him watching her, she had turned her head the other way. She was facing the other way now, even though he was sure she had seen him coming. Billy Nathan had seen her kind before—women who thought they were way above the likes of him in importance and station. He smiled, assuring himself that she would think differently in just a few moments.

The skinny youth walked toward the porch with a determined stride. He noticed that the pudgy older man in the checkered suit and derby hat was now watching him, a kind of curious expression on his face. Billy Nathan decided that the man was a peddler, from the looks of him, and that was good, too, for peddlers got around a lot

and they talked a lot. This one would have the story of
Billy Nathan to talk about.

When he was eight or ten paces from the porch and
the man who was still slowly rocking in the chair, Billy
Nathan stopped. "You," he called, the word carrying as
much menace as he could manage.

The man he had addressed kept rocking, not missing
one back-and-forth beat. He appeared not to have heard—or
almost, for the clasped hands unclasped slowly, the right
one edging just an inch toward the gun strapped to his
thigh. But the hat over the man's eyes stayed exactly
where it was.

"I'm talkin' to you!" Billy Nathan shouted. "You, Rado
Kane! Or should I call you *Col-o-ray-do*?"

The chair's motion abruptly stopped. With his left
forefinger, the man slowly pushed the brim of his hat back
on his head. The face that was uncovered was almost
expressionless, but the pale blue eyes regarding Billy were
narrowed and cold.

"Maybe you shouldn't call me anything."

There was a flatness to the voice, a kind of deadliness,
that drove a stake of ice down Billy's backbone. It was the
kind of tone he himself had tried to project but had not
come close to.

He shook off the feeling of dread, reminding himself
that anybody could talk tough; backing it up was what
counted. Squaring his shoulders, he said in as steely a
voice as he could muster, "I'm calling you out, is what.
That's what I'm doing, Mr. Rado Kane."

To his left there was sudden movement. Taking his
eyes from the man he had just challenged, the youth saw
that the peddler had taken both women by the arms and
was moving them farther down the porch, away from the
man in the rocking chair. He laughed to himself. He had
their attention now, all right, including the pretty young
woman's.

"No need to worry, ma'am," he said with a leering
grin. "Billy Nathan hits only what he aims at." He wished

he had worn his hat this morning, just so he could have taken it off and bowed to her in a mocking kind of way. Well, he could not think of everything in advance, not on a day like this.

The man in the chair nodded. "Billy Nathan," he uttered in the same flat voice he had used before.

"You heard of me?" Billy asked with a smirk.

"Can't say as I have."

"But I have," a gruff voice declared from behind Billy. "Keep your hands where I can see them, boy. And make all your moves slow ones."

Following orders, Billy turned around slowly and found that Sam Loomis was now down off the stage box and was standing a few feet away. The youth also found that he was staring at the business end of the guard's sawed-off shotgun, which was trained right at his stomach.

"Let me tell you about Billy Nathan," Loomis announced, his eyes staring into the youth's and his voice directed at Rado Kane. "He's built himself a minor reputation as a gunhand 'cause he's pretty good at shootin' younger boys and old drunks. What's your count now, Billy? Four, maybe five?"

"They were all fair fights!" Billy snarled. "You don't know nothin' about nothin'! If you didn't have that gun on me—"

"But I do," Loomis countered. "Which ends it. It ends right here, Billy Nathan—that is, unless you want to call for a messier finish."

Jabbing his thumb over his shoulder at the porch behind him, the youth demanded, "What about him? What about Rado Kane? He's done more'n his share of killin'. I know all about him from up in the Colorado Territory. Well, this mornin' he's met his match. Me! Billy Nathan! And it don't make no difference if you stop me, 'cause if I don't get him here, I'll get him someplace else. I know where this stage is goin' and—"

"Put away the shotgun," Rado Kane suddenly called.

Billy wheeled around. The rocking chair still rocked,

but it was empty, for Kane now stood beside it, facing the young gunfighter.

Checking over his shoulder, Billy was relieved to find the shotgun guard lowering his weapon.

"Kane?" Loomis asked in a bewildered voice. "The passenger list says Smith."

A half-smile formed on Kane's face. "Sometimes it works, and other times people have the good sense to leave things be." He stepped off the porch onto the dusty road. "Obviously this isn't one of those times."

Loomis moved forward and assessed his passenger. After a long moment, he remarked, "There don't have to be trouble here this mornin', Mr. Kane."

Kane shook his head. "Like Billy says, if not here, someplace else." Then he stared at his young challenger. "I take it you mean that, boy?"

"You're damned right I do!" Billy answered, and without warning his hand dived for his pistol grip.

But he was not fast enough, for his Colt had yet to clear leather when the slug from Kane's gun smashed into Billy's right shoulder, the force slamming him to the ground. He lay there stunned, his vision blurred, and then he tried to shake his head to clear it. Suddenly Kane's boot smashed into the skinny youth's body, spinning him onto his stomach. But he quickly forgot about the pain from that blow as Kane's boot was planted firmly on his right wrist, causing a wrenching pain in his shoulder. Then he saw Kane's gun barrel only inches away from his right hand.

"No!" Nathan screamed, and then the scream turned into a crazed shriek as Kane's gun exploded and the bullet smashed the bones in Billy's hand. Blackness took Nathan before he could feel anything more.

"That was unnecessarily brutal!" a woman's horrified voice proclaimed to Rado Kane.

Turning toward the voice, Kane looked briefly at the young woman on the porch, who was staring at him in disbelief. Then he reached down to pull the Colt from

Billy's holster, and as he shoved the gun under his own gun belt he glanced at Sam Loomis. "Looks like the boy needs a doctor," the gunfighter told the shotgunner. With a slight shrug, he added, "Could just as easily have been an undertaker."

As the stage rolled eastward out of Yuma, Crystal Richmond pushed herself into the corner of the seat and silently assessed the two men across from her and the woman to her left—her fellow travelers and companions for at least part of her journey across the Arizona desert. All three of them had their hats pulled down over their eyes and appeared completely relaxed. Crystal shuddered to herself, appalled that they were behaving as if nothing at all had happened back there at the station—nothing at all. She wondered again whether she had made a terrible mistake in coming out to Arizona Territory—and wondered also if she would ever come to understand the rugged land and its people.

She turned Rado Kane's name over in her mind a few times. She had never heard it before, and she did not know if Lyman Whisters had. Her gaze lingered on the peddler, recalling how he had introduced himself: "Lyman Whisters, purveyor of fine liquors and even finer liqueurs, who most unfortunately has drawn the Arizona Territory as his selling area." The shotgun guard certainly seemed to have heard of Kane, and she thought Walt Grader, the driver, had also.

As for the older woman, Crystal did not know whether the gunfighter's name had meant anything to her or not. The woman had said not a word to her or to anybody else all morning—not even introducing herself. Maybe she had heard of Rado Kane and maybe not. The boy who had been shot certainly had.

Rado Kane. The name meant nothing to Crystal. Well, after all, she was coming from California. No doubt he had not yet had the time to establish himself as a legend there.

Brutal, unnecessarily so. That is what she had declared his actions to be, and it was true. She had never seen anything like it before; but then, she had never seen a real duel with guns before—not like this one. True, San Francisco had had its share of brutality, and she had seen guns being used, as well as sudden death when someone was caught cheating at cards or when a woman came between two men. Unlike the Chicago she had left over a year ago, life out West seemed very cheap. Civilized society, where it existed, was little more than a veneer that covered a coarse barbarism, even in San Francisco. But what she had witnessed in Yuma a short while before chilled her to the bone.

Yes, the youth had begun things, but the shotgun guard had had the trouble well in hand. Kane had demanded the fight with someone he did not even know and someone who was little more than a boy. And then for Kane to have permanently maimed his challenger after he had won . . . She shivered involuntarily.

What was it Whisters had said directly after the shooting? "Welcome to the Arizona Territory, miss. Not too many people out here, and from what you've just seen, you'll no doubt conclude that's not a bad thing."

"And Tucson?" she had asked him. "Is it like this in Tucson?"

The peddler had smiled. "Well, I suppose the best thing you can say about Tucson is that though it isn't much, it's growing—and at least you'll find a semblance of law and order there."

Now, staring out the window of the stage, she tried to imagine the place she was heading for and found that she could not.

"Miss?"

The voice broke off her daydreaming. Turning her head, she found the salesman staring at her and realized he had been saying something. She tried to erase the worried expression on her face as she said to him, "I'm sorry, Mr. Whisters. I'm afraid I didn't hear you."

The liquor peddler had been using a full and heavy-looking red-and-green-checkered cloth bag as a pillow. Pulling it from behind his neck, he held it on his lap as he smiled back and remarked, "I was saying that I hope you don't think I'm prying, but I was wondering why it is you're going to Tucson. I'm assuming that's where you're headed, since you asked about it." He held up his forefinger to make a point, adding, "Please understand, I'm not wanting to stick my nose where it doesn't belong, but trips like this can get pretty long if there's no conversation. If you want to talk about something else, that's fine. For example, I could tell you my life story, but that would be extremely boring. You can believe me. I've heard it . . . several times."

The good-natured twinkle in the man's eyes made Crystal laugh in spite of herself. "I'm sure your life story is much more interesting than mine, Mr. Whisters." Seizing the opportunity, she turned to the other woman. "Yours, too, no doubt, Mrs.—"

The woman stirred, reached up, and took the straw hat from her head. "It's Hallan, Isabel Hallan. And life stories are what you make them to be," the elderly passenger remarked in a measured voice. "If the life isn't worth much itself, you can always give lie to the story. Most folks do." She looked disapprovingly at Whisters, then went on. "If I was to speculate, I'd guess a whiskey drummer's lies would be better than most." That said, she replaced the hat and settled back into her corner, making it very clear she wanted no further conversation.

Whisters laughed uncomfortably, then cleared his throat and declared to the young woman seated across from him, "Well, that leaves just the two of us, seeing as how Mr. Kane appears to be sleeping, so I suppose the first order of business is to determine who goes first. If I may, I propose that such determination be simplified through the powers invested in these ever-useful cards of chance. Simply pick one. The holder of the high card shall be our first orator."

As if by magic, a deck of playing cards had appeared

in Whisters's hands and were now fanned before Crystal, their red backs facing her. She hesitated, then drew one: the queen of hearts.

"Now, if you'll kindly draw one for me," Whisters suggested.

The young woman chose again, drawing the three of spades. She then returned both cards, and the deck vanished as quickly and mysteriously as it had appeared.

With a sigh, Crystal began, "Chicago. That's where I grew up."

"Really? A nice city in its way."

"You've been there?"

Whisters smiled. "There are few places I haven't been, I'd hazard to guess. But this is your story, not mine. When did you leave . . . and why?"

"About a year ago. I—well, you see, I sing and dance, and in Chicago there are a lot of young women who do those things and do them very well. Not that I don't think I do, too, you understand, but it seemed to me that if I went somewhere where there was less competition, I could enjoy a greater success. San Francisco seemed like the right place, from all I'd heard about it, so that's where I went."

"But it wasn't the right place?"

She was silent for a long moment, staring down at her hands, then said softly, "There were jobs, plenty of them, for the people there are eager for Eastern-style entertainment. But—oh, dear, I'm not sure I know how to say this."

Whisters leaned forward and put his hand on Crystal's. "I've been in San Francisco, Miss Richmond. I know what kind of place it can be. I also know that there aren't a lot of—er—handsome women there. But there *are* a lot of men."

Crystal's laugh had a bitter edge to it. "A lot of men, yes, most of whom didn't much care about the quality of your singing or dancing. The key to your popularity and success had more to do with the costume you wore"—she sniffed derisively—"or should I say the *amount* of costume, for the smaller the better."

"But you stayed a year."

Her hazel eyes took on a pained look, and her hands played nervously with the lace handkerchief she had been using to dab away sweat. "Yes. I thought everybody had to start out that way—you know, work your way to recognition for your talent and your qualities." She laughed bitterly again. "And I did achieve recognition—except the qualities that drew the kind of sponsorship I needed weren't the ones I had had in mind." She shook her head, then forced a smile. "So I left for something better."

"For Tucson."

"Yes. I know a woman there, an older woman, who left San Francisco about six months ago. She runs a saloon in Tucson but has recently come into some money, and she wants to turn her place into a proper theater and wrote asking me if I was interested." Her face brightened. "My friend's letter came at precisely the right time."

Lyman Whisters nodded. "Well, Tucson certainly could use a good theater. Lord knows it's got enough saloons, so one less won't hurt that town a bit." He doffed his hat and smiled warmly. "Here's to your good fortune, Miss Richmond."

Crystal thanked him, then declared, "There, that's my tale. Now let me hear your story."

Chuckling, the peddler remarked, "It's one easily told, for I've lived my life selling. I've sold a lot of different things in a lot of different places. Not wanting to brag, but in the spirit of complete honesty, I happen to be a very good salesman." He gestured expansively, saying, "The most enjoyable part of my work is that it's enabled me to meet a lot of interesting people, and I expect I'll meet a lot more. I've had my high moments, and I've experienced the low, but all in all it's not been a bad life, by my reckoning. And that's the only reckoning that counts—I think."

He smiled broadly, his brown eyes twinkling in his

pudgy face, and again the deck of cards appeared in his hand. "Now, if I can have your complete and undivided attention, I'd like to demonstrate for you one or two examples of an avocation of mine—what might in fact be called my second profession." Leaning over, he dealt five cards to Crystal and five to himself. "Now, look at your cards; turn them faceup."

When she did, she was looking at a pair of jacks and a two, a four, and an eight of different suits. Whisters's cards, now also faceup, were a pair of queens and three similar small, unmatched numbers.

"All right," the peddler declared, "naturally you'll hold on to your jacks and I'll keep my queens, which means you'll take three new cards and so will I."

He dealt the six cards facedown. "Now, let's have a look at what you have."

Crystal smiled at the four jacks and the ten in her new hand and displayed them to her companion. "I seem to have been lucky," she said.

Whisters nodded agreement. "Lucky enough to bet your future, one might think. And one would be right . . . almost." He turned over his three new cards.

Crystal exhaled in astonishment at four queens and an ace.

Suddenly Rado Kane grunted, and Crystal's eyes moved from the salesman to the gunfighter. Kane's hat was off now, and he had been watching the card game. Crystal blushed, thinking not about the cards but remembering the things she had told Lyman Whisters about her life, completely forgetting the presence of her fellow passenger.

"Saw a man in west Kansas do that same trick," Kane declared laconically. "Only he did it in the middle of a real poker game." He paused dramatically, then added, "He got his left ear shot off for his payoff."

Eyeing the gunfighter, the young woman responded stiffly, "No doubt, Mr. Kane, you have seen more than your share of such things."

"That could be—and if you stay out here, you will,

too. And if you start using those card tricks, you'll probably have a use for this—that is, unless you already have
one of your own." He was offering Billy Nathan's gun to
her, holding it by the barrel.

Shaking her head disdainfully, she retorted, "Thank
you, but I don't believe a young woman has need of such a
thing—be it in Chicago or Tucson, Mr. Kane." The frost
in her tone seemed to cool the coach interior by several
degrees.

Kane appeared not to notice. "You're not in Tucson
yet, miss, and between here and there it's possible some
folks similar to Billy Nathan could show up and menace
you. In any case, being prepared can't hurt." He reached
over and placed the gun on the seat beside her, but she
ignored it and stared out the window.

Shifting in his seat, Whisters hoped he could take
some of the frost off the conversation and restore a friendly
atmosphere to the coach. He turned to his seatmate and
asked, "Er, Mr. Kane, are you traveling to Tucson as
well?"

"No, just about halfway. A town called Gila Bend.
Got a job to do there," Kane answered.

Whisters nodded and decided to give the young woman
another try. "Despite it's being pronounced *Hee-la,* it's
spelled G-I-L-A, like the lizard," he pointed out. "But the
town actually takes the first part of its name from the Gila
River, which abruptly changes course just north of town—
and that explains the second part of its name."

Obviously softening, Crystal remarked, "You said 'like
the lizard.' I'm afraid I don't know what creature you're
referring to."

Smiling at her improved mood, Whisters explained,
"The full name is Gila monster. It's a fat lizard, about two
feet in length, and it's colored in kind of alternating orange and brown squares"—he chuckled—"not unlike my
suit. It can be very dangerous if not left alone, since it's
poisonous. But it doesn't kill like a rattlesnake—you know,
sinking its fangs and injecting its venom all at once. What

it has to do is chew on its victim for a time so that its poison can slowly enter the bloodstream."

"Ugh!" Crystal exclaimed. "How gruesome!" She immediately turned her attention back out the window.

Mentally kicking himself for having gone too far, the peddler turned back to Rado Kane. "Have you been to Gila Bend before?" he asked pleasantly.

"No."

"Are you planning to stay long?"

Kane shook his head slightly. "Nope. Just in and out. The job I've been hired to do shouldn't take all that much time." The gunfighter then placed his hat over his eyes and settled back on the leather seat.

Whisters sighed. Kane had retreated under his hat, Crystal was staring blankly out the window, and Mrs. Hallan sat virtually unmoving with downcast eyes, obviously not wishing to socialize. *The life of a salesman can be a trying one at times*, the peddler told himself, *not to mention exceedingly boring*.

Chapter Two

"**O**kay, folks," Walt Grader called down from the driver's box as he pulled the horses to a stop, "you've got a few minutes at this here way station. We change horses here, we eat here, and we take care of what the stage line likes us to call our matters of personal hygiene. After that, we'll pull out precisely on schedule, and I'll let you know when that is." He hopped down from the box and pulled open the door, then smiled at the travelers inside. "Welcome to Adonde!"

"Where?" Crystal Richmond asked as she alighted from the stage and stood with her three fellow passengers on the gravelly earth, staring at the small corral filled with horses and the lone small adobe building in front of which the stage had halted. As the corral and the home station building were all that existed on the dry landscape for as far as the eye could see in any direction, they might well have been the only things on the entire face of the earth.

"Look around, and I'm sure you'll see how the place got its name," Lyman Whisters quipped. "*Adonde* is Spanish for 'where.' Probably the first time anyone was ever welcomed here, the one being welcomed was so taken with its—er—splendor that '¿*Adonde?*' was his or her incredulous response."

Rado Kane nodded as he wiped the sweat from his neck with a red plaid bandanna. "The best *adonde* would be inside, out of the heat."

Needing no further encouragement, the passengers, as well as Sam Loomis, hurried into the cooler interior of the station, while Walt Grader went to change the horses. There was not much in the way of accommodation, but waiting for them at a small, cramped table was a hot stack of flat tortillas served with beans and a spicy red sauce. A pitcher of cold well water was brought to them by the stationmaster, a man Loomis called simply Bush. Looking as if he could be anywhere from his late sixties to early nineties, there was no doubt the man took his name from his dingy white tobacco-stained beard, its unruly curls hiding most of his lower face and extending almost the width of his narrow shoulders.

"We need to talk," the old man muttered to the shotgun guard, gesturing with his rifle toward the outside. When Loomis rose and headed toward the open doorway, Kane did the same.

When they had gone, Isabel Hallan reached into her carpetbag and retrieved her length of wire. Her remaining fellow passengers watched in fascination as the woman began to twirl it between her hands as she had done at the Yuma station earlier.

The elderly widow's face was expressionless, her eyes seemingly unfocused, as though she were in some kind of trance. Crystal and Whisters exchanged glances, although the young woman was clearly far more puzzled than the peddler. Whisters stared silently until the rotating loop had stopped its motion and the wire was back in the woman's bag. "That looks like a piano wire," he commented.

Mrs. Hallan nodded, then said simply, "What it looks like, it is."

"It's none of my business, but have you been using it very long?" the salesman queried.

For the first time during the entire journey, the older woman smiled. It was not a broad smile, but there was a hint of friendliness about it. "It *is* none of your business, Mr. Whisters, you are right," she replied, her blue eyes twinkling mischievously. "But yes, I have been using the wire for a good long time. I have been doing *everything* for a good long time. Odd, though, that you would know about it. Not many people do."

Whisters laughed. "I know a few things, I guess, but I see a lot more. And I admit I've only seen one other person use the wire. A gentleman in Sacramento. He was known as being very accurate."

"I've had my accurate times, too," the widow declared, and the light went out of her eyes as they again became slightly unfocused.

Crystal could not contain her curiosity any longer and asked in an imploring voice, "Please, will one of you—or both of you—tell me what you're talking about?"

Mrs. Hallan looked at her, then at Whisters. She nodded toward the salesman, deferring to him.

Clearing his throat, the peddler said, "Well, I'll tell you about the man in Sacramento. He used what he called the vibrations of the piano wire to tune his mind to things and to people. He could make some very accurate predictions based on the feelings he got."

"You mean he was a fortune teller?" Crystal asked, startled.

"That's not what he called himself," Whisters replied. "He called himself by some newfangled name—a psychic. I don't know what the difference is, if any; but then, I don't know all that much about it. Perhaps that's something Mrs. Hallan might explain to us."

The old woman's smile was full now as she turned to Crystal. "I might, but I won't. What you call something doesn't really matter. Some people think it does, but I don't."

"You were, well, reading it—if that's what you call it—just now," Crystal pointed out. "Did you get any messages or feelings or . . ." The young woman's puzzled voice trailed off.

Mrs. Hallan's smile was gone. "I felt a number of things, yes." She was looking out the open doorway through which the three men had passed. "Mr. Bush," she murmured slowly. "He should be careful. Very careful."

The men had stopped by the small corral. Bush looked at Kane's face, then at his gun, and then at Loomis.

"Mr. Kane's bein' here is all right," the shotgunner quickly assured the stationmaster.

Bush nodded to himself as he stroked his thick beard. "I heard tell of some bandits to the east," he said finally. "Mexicans, new to the territory, far as I can tell. Probably after silver mine payroll money. You carryin' any?"

Loomis shook his head. "Not this trip. But we heard about the Mexicans in Yuma. Apparently they're a ragtag bunch, led by somebody called Morales. Not much of a gang, from what we know of 'em, but it'll pay to keep our eyes peeled."

Rado Kane had been regarding the shotgunner intently, then remarked, "I notice you didn't want to mention this to the other passengers. Is that a stage-line policy?"

Loomis grinned, and his weathered, craggy face softened. "Nope, it's a Sam Loomis policy. I figure there's no sense havin' anybody's nerves all frazzled before there's a need." He chuckled, then added, "But now that you know, Mr. Kane, you can start gettin' just as nervous as you like."

"He'll have company in that," Bush said. "You got a new passenger who's been waitin' here, and he's as jumpy as a lizard in a fry pan. Been that way since he rode in early this mornin'."

Bush used his rifle to point to a tired-looking piebald inside the corral. "I gave him ten dollars for his horse and saddle, but I doubt I'll get that much sellin' it."

The man the stationmaster was talking about stood by himself to the rear of the adobe building. Tall, thin almost to the point of skeletal, he wore a black bowler hat and black frock coat, both of which seemed at least a size too big. Kane judged him to be in his mid-forties, and he agreed that the man appeared to be ill at ease. "Looks like a preacher," he observed.

"That's exactly what he claims," Bush confirmed. "And that's the way he's been since he got here, just like you see him. Pacin' back and forth, clutchin' that black satchel bag of his, and lookin' back toward Yuma from where he rode in, like he's worried about somebody bein' after him. Had me gettin' a little jumpy myself, he did"—he patted the rifle cradled in the crook of his arm—"such that I kept Old Peaceful right nearby all day."

The rifle was a well-oiled 1866 model Winchester .44. Behind the forward handgrip was an elaborately engraved forest scene depicting some sort of antlered animal with an oddly bloated body.

"What's that supposed to be?" the gunfighter asked Bush, gazing at the animal.

"Don't rightly know. I've given it some thought from time to time, and I reckon it's an elk that got pregnant by mistake." Bush snorted. "'Course, it'd have to be a *real* mistake, since *he's* wearin' them antlers. Or maybe it's really a pregnant female who's wearin' them antlers as a *dis*guise." The old man then cackled at what Kane guessed to be a joke he had told many times. Falling suddenly silent, Bush peered at the younger man through narrowed, watery eyes, challenging, "Unless you got a better idea?"

Kane shrugged. "It's your gun."

Loomis then tapped Kane on the shoulder, saying, "We'll be headin' out shortly, so we'd best get inside and have some grub before it's too late." He glanced over at the stage, where Grader was checking the rigging of the new team, adding, "By now, you probably know how Walt likes to be prompt, and he's almost finished, so we'll be out of here inside of ten minutes." He chuckled. "It takes him less time to eat than any man I've ever seen."

It was exactly nine minutes later when Grader gave the order for all passengers to board. Kane took a few moments to use the privy, and by the time he had reached the coach the women and the peddler were already seated on the front-facing rear seat, and the new passenger was seated on the front seat under the driver. Kane sat down beside him.

"My name is Cull, the Reverend Gideon Cull," the wraithlike man announced to his fellow traveler. "I am a traveling servant of the Lord God Almighty." He then extended his hand toward Rado Kane, but the gunfighter was busy adjusting his gun belt so that his revolver rested on the top of his thigh rather than the side.

The stage lurched suddenly forward, causing the reverend to momentarily lose his composure—and his balance —but once the coach settled into its normal pitching roll, Cull returned his attention to Kane. "I've already met our other three colleagues of the road. But you are, sir . . . ?"

Kane studied the man's face, which was long and pinched with thin curled lips. The dark brown eyes above the long, narrow nose seemed to dart, never staying focused on the same place. The face, and the man's habit of rubbing his hands together, were at odds with the mellow tone of his voice, and the effect was something like a leather glove caressing a satin dress.

"My name is Kane," the gunfighter finally replied tersely. Then he pulled his hat over his eyes and slouched down into the seat.

"Mr. Kane is not a man of conversation," Crystal Richmond informed the newcomer.

Kane tipped up the edge of his hat brim to look at her, and she in turn was looking at him. There was no malice in her eyes, as there had been none in her tone, just a matter-of-fact look to match the matter-of-fact comment. Grunting, Kane pulled the brim back down.

"Well, not everyone is gifted at everything," Cull observed. "The way I like to put it, every single one of the Lord's creatures has his or her—or its—role to play in God's grand design. My special calling, or my mission in life, is interpreting the Lord's Word to those who have need of it. Which, in truth, is all of us."

Shifting his attention to the length of wire Mrs. Hallan was twirling in her hands, Cull looked sharply at the widow and asked, "What, may I ask, *is* that thing?"

"It's an A-string," the elderly woman replied, as if that were all the explanation needed. There was an edge to her voice, and her eyes were narrowed as they looked at the preacher. "Some people use tea leaves, others cards, others read palms. I use an A-string from a piano."

"To do what?" Cull demanded stiffly. "To tell the fortunes of the gullible?"

Mrs. Hallan smiled. "As you said, Reverend Cull, we all have our special callings."

"Some," the preacher intoned haughtily, "are not without fault in the eyes of the Lord."

He coughed, then brightened as he turned to Crystal. "However, as we shall be traveling together for a time, I would be delighted, Miss Richmond—and you too, of course, Mrs. Hallan—to counsel you on fruitful passages of the Good Book that you might find of particular value." Taking in the beauty of the young woman, he added, "I would also be happy to give you the benefit of more specific counsel on matters of a more personal nature, should you wish."

He then smiled thinly at the two men—despite the fact that Kane's eyes were covered by his hat. "I have Bibles here in my satchel that you gentlemen might like to read as well. As we cross this desert of desolation you might find comfort in the recorded yearnings that the early Hebrews—God's chosen people—had for just such a burned-out place. You may recall that they pleaded with the mighty Pharaoh of Egypt, 'Let us go, we pray thee, three days' journey into the desert, and sacrifice unto the Lord our God, lest he fall upon us with pestilence, or with the sword.'" He paused, then instructed, "You will find that plea in Exodus, chapter five, verse three."

Cull extended a bony index finger toward heaven—or at least to the roof of the coach—and remarked, "The story of Pharaoh and the Hebrews' wish to depart Egypt is one

from which we all can gain many insights into the work-
ings of the Lord. And, in the person of mighty Pharaoh,
we have an unsurpassed example of what can happen to
one who thinks himself above God's holy laws."

Kane snorted, and he again tipped up the brim of his
hat. "Fortune smiles upon you, Miss Richmond. One of
your fellow passengers can teach you card tricks to get you
shot at, another can teach you how to shoot back, and
when you miss, this one can argue to get your soul into
heaven."

"What makes you think I'd miss?" Crystal asked angrily.

"Let's call it an educated hunch," Kane retorted. "And
if you'd like better proof than that, ask Mrs. Hallan to spin
her wire."

Two hours after the stagecoach had left the Adonde
station, a lone rider on a dun-colored mare approached
the adobe building slowly from the west. Now walking,
both horse and man looked as though they had had a hard
ride—and as if life in general was not treating them all too
kindly. The mare's ribs showed clearly through a scruffy,
lathered coat, reflecting both scant feeding and poor groom-
ing, and the rider was clothed in torn and frayed denim
pants and jacket, while his hat, of undeterminable color,
was torn in several places.

Beneath the hat brim, straw-colored hair descended
in matted, gnarled knots. The face was young—that of a
man in his early twenties at most—and the odd, staring
quality of his pale yellow-green eyes gave him the look of
someone either half-idiot or half-mad or both. From the
tattered cuffs of his too-short jacket protruded bony wrists
that ended in long, tapering fingers. Those of the left hand
loosely fondled the horse's reins, while the fingers of the
other hand drummed, seemingly thoughtlessly, on the
chipped butt of the fifteen-year-old Remington-Beals Army
revolver in the scarred leather holster that flapped loosely
on the young man's thin thigh.

But Judd Neep's head was full of thoughts, all focused

on a particular target: one solitary man of all those the Lord had seen fit to put on earth from the time of Adam till now—the Reverend Gideon Cull.

As he and the mare made their slow progress toward the station, Judd's eyes took in the corral, and a slight smile suddenly formed on his lips at the sight of the familiar horse, which he knew for certain was the preacher's. Trust in the Lord, Cull liked to say. Well, Judd had done just as the man had said . . . and the Lord had shown him the right way to take. If Gideon Cull, with all his self-appointed saintliness, had been asking heaven to throw his pursuer off his trail, heaven sure was not going out of its way to help.

And now, if the Lord had seen fit to make the stage late or to have Cull miss it, Judd Neep would see just how much the preacher trusted that same Lord.

As he stepped up to the porch of the station building, the old stationmaster came outside, a rifle cradled in his arm. He looked at the young visitor and assessed him briefly. "Afternoon."

"Good afternoon," Judd replied in an even, friendly voice. "I'm hopin' to catch the stage to Tucson."

Stroking his beard, Bush informed him, "Too late. It left a couple of hours ago."

Judd Neep smiled as pleasantly as he could. "I guess that means I gotta keep ridin'. But I need some water. Me and my horse both."

"Got plenty of water." Gesturing at the horse, the old man declared, "Looks like the mare could use more than that, though. She's welcome to some feed, and I can scrape up a plate of beans for you, if you like."

"I'd be much obliged," the young man responded, still smiling. He looked around, then asked, "You here all by yourself?"

The old man's eyes narrowed. "Just me and Old Peaceful, here. Why'd you ask?"

Shrugging, Judd answered lightly, "Just makin' conversation. Comin' in here, the place looked real lonely, that's all. Would help to have somebody around to talk to, is what I was thinkin'."

"I get about all the talk I need, son. Now, you want them beans or what?"

"First things first," Judd said, nodding toward his horse.

Under Bush's watchful eye, the youth led the mare into the corral, watered the horse, then took a long drink himself from the well bucket. Suddenly he pointed at the other horse standing lazily at the far end of the corral. "That piebald there. I'm pretty sure he belongs to someone I know. A preacher. He take the stage out today?"

The old man nodded. "If you're aimin' to meet up with him, you might want to buy his horse. Yours looks like she could use a rest."

Judd smiled again. "The Reverend Cull likes to say there ain't no rest for them with the Lord's work to do. But you're right. I'll take the horse."

Bush nodded, then remarked, "Good. I sure don't have no use for it. Make you a real fair price."

Grinning, the youth countered, "I didn't figure on payin' an *unfair* price, mister. You gonna throw that saddle in, too?"

The old stationmaster turned and looked at the preacher's saddle, which was mounted on the corral fence. "I don't see why not. 'Pears to be a lot better than the one you—"

He abruptly stopped speaking at the sound of Judd's pistol being cocked. Pivoting on his heel, he snapped the Winchester up to firing position, but it was too late. The bullet from Judd Neep's Remington smashed into Bush's face to the right of his nose, and he went down in a bloodied heap.

Judd emptied two more shells into the already dead man's head. "One bullet was a fair price, old man," he quipped, still grinning. "But two more'll cinch the deal, I figure."

Within half an hour the young killer was riding east-ward, feeling better than he had felt in days. Astride the preacher's piebald, he looked back at the saddled mare following behind and thought to himself, *Rode in with one horse, rode out with two. Rode in with one old pistol, rode out with two pistols and a dandy-fine Winchester, complete with tooled scabbard. Rode in thirsty and hungry, rode out with beans in the belly, more in the saddlebags, and two full canteens of water. Yep. Worth three bullets any day.*

But now there was more riding to be done to accomplish his mission. He had heard Gideon Cull say numerous times, "We each have our own mission, our own individual special calling, that's ours and nobody else's." Then the preacher always added just what his mission was—at that particular moment.

"It's my mission, boy, to get you out of this terrible fix you're in." That is what the Reverend Gideon Cull had told Judd Neep the very first time they had met more than six months earlier in Ehrenberg. Judd had come out of the saloon at about four in the afternoon, and it was as if the preacher had been waiting outside the swinging doors especially for him.

"I ain't in no terrible fix," he had protested to Cull. "I ain't in no fix at all." He had laughed and had started to walk away from the stern-looking man, when the preacher forcefully grabbed his sleeve and pulled him back. The combination of the sudden pull, the drinks he had had, and the heat of the day had made Judd stagger slightly.

"You see? That's part of the fix you're in," the preacher had solemnly declared. "Drunkenness leads to ruin. The other part of your fix is this town. What's your name, boy?"

The youth had told him.

"Well, Judd Neep, this is one of the most evil places I have ever laid eyes upon since I began my service to the

Lord. Whores and gamblers and cheats, and more cheats and more gamblers and more whores! There's not an honest businessman in the whole of the town."

"Mr. Greeber is," Judd had argued. "He's honest, and I'm honest, too. That's why I work in his warehouse, and sometimes I even haul freight for him. Why, I've been as far east as Prescott." He had thought to himself that if the preacher wanted to see his fill of whores and gamblers, he might better go there. But the young man did not tell Cull that. The preacher never gave him the chance.

"How old are you, boy?"

"I'll be nineteen in the spring."

"Nineteen," Cull had repeated, as if weighing the word carefully. "And what is your mission, Judd Neep?"

"My what?"

"Your mission, your special calling. Your service to the Lord. Don't you know He demands service from us all?" The preacher shook his head, and his long, lank dark hair flapped behind his ears. "No, I don't suppose you do know much about that. Do you attend religious services regularly?"

Judd had scratched his head. "Can't say it's been regular, I guess."

"How about your Bible reading? How often do you consult the Holy Word of God?"

That one was easier. "I don't read much," he had admitted.

"You mean you don't read at all."

Flushing, Judd had angrily responded, "Wait a minute! What right have you got to—"

"Every right, Judd, every right there is," Cull had cut in, a sad look on his cadaverous face. "Because that's my mission. *You're* my mission."

"Suppose I don't want to be no mission—yours or anybody else's?" the youth had obstinately retorted.

"Suppose, Judd boy, that there was profit in it?"

"Profit?"

"Learning to read, for one thing. When I get done teaching you, you'll be reading God's Word for your very own self."

Judd had considered the prospect, then shrugged. "I done all right without readin', so far."

"Then, of course, there's the money." The preacher had paused meaningfully.

"What money?"

Cull had smiled, which merely imparted a sinister aspect to his skeletal face. "The money that people give us—you and me—to continue doing the Lord's work. Why, they'll come to our tent in droves to hear God's message—as you and I speak it—and they will rejoice! And, in their rejoicing, they'll beg us to take their coins of gold and silver. They'll do that, Judd boy, so that you and I can continue on, working to spread this joy through our message to others in need of it."

Judd had thought for a moment, then shook his head in bewilderment. "I don't get this message part. I ain't got no message."

"You surely do, boy," the preacher had insisted. "You've been saved. Saved! You heard the very word from the Reverend Gideon Cull, and you put away childish things. You put behind you your evil drinking and whoring ways, and you accepted the Lord's way. Your message will be one of personal conversion."

"But I ain't had no personal conversion," the young man had pointed out.

"You will, Judd—if you join me. If I say you're converted, you are. And if you say so, you are. It's as simple as that."

Stubbornly, Judd had persisted, "But this message—I still don't know what it might be."

The preacher had grinned. "We will rehearse that, Judd. We will rehearse it over and over again, and you will come to know it in your sleep."

The very next night, after a full day of rehearsing, Judd Neep had indeed delivered his message. There were

only about twenty people in the tent—all men—but even
the ones who had seemed drunk listened when the young
man stood up and gave his talk. He knew every word by
heart: "I was lost in whiskey," he had told the audience. "I
was lost in the temp-ta-tions of the flesh. I spent all my
time with the whoresome women of sin or with the mind-
rotting bottle of Satan's brew. I—"

"*All* your time?" someone had interrupted. "Ain't you
the kid who works down at Greeber's? Sure you are! I
seen you down there."

Judd had swallowed hard. There were not supposed
to have been any interruptions. Then the preacher's voice
had suddenly rung out, "Right you are, brother! Right you
are! Judd, here, had a good job, a decent job. And what
did he do with his money? As he was telling us, he was
spending it on wickedness—the very wickedness that, had
he continued, would have lost him his very mind and
thereby his job that provided him the money he was
spending. This world is a place of endless cycles, friend.
But God came to Judd Neep's rescue." He had turned to
the youth and smiled benevolently. "Judd boy, tell us
how."

The young man had smiled blankly back. He had lost
his place.

"Judd . . ."

"I was lost in whiskey," he had repeated. "I was lost
in the temp-ta-tions of the flesh. I spent all my time with
the whoresome women of sin or with the mind-rotting
bottle of Satan's—"

A man's voice had broken in, shouting, "You said that
already!"

Indeed he had, word for word. But that was the way
he had learned it. He closed his eyes and murmured
under his breath, "Satan's brew, Satan's brew." Yes, that
was it. "And then"—Ah! He had located his place again!
—"then the Reverend Gideon Cull found me. He found
me in the street. I was alone, I was sick, I was deep in sin.
And the Reverend showed me God!"

Opening his eyes, the young man had inhaled deeply. His message was complete. He had breathed out with relief and sat down.

"What a blessing!" the preacher had extolled jubilantly. "What a blessing indeed has come to this town of Ehrenberg. A young man has been saved from a sinful life. A soul has been saved from eternal damnation. Spread this word, my brothers. Tomorrow evening Judd Neep will again bear witness to the Lord's blessing. Let the multitude rejoice here with him now . . . and tomorrow evening!"

And rejoice they had. Everybody had shouted and clapped the young convert on the back, making him feel good. He had felt even better the next night when a real crowd showed up—women and children, as well as men—and if anybody had been wise to the fact that his message was identical to the one the night before, not a word had been said. And afterward, Cull showed him what the crowd had left in his hat.

When Gideon Cull had shown his new recruit what had been given as offerings, Judd had been amazed. He had never figured that anybody could get that many pieces of gold and silver for such little work. The preacher had been right: Spreading God's Word paid off well.

They had spread the Word in Ehrenberg for a little more than three weeks when Cull decided they should be moving on, since the number of people coming to the tent was growing increasingly smaller. The night before they left he added another reason. "Do you remember Sarah Leffler?" the preacher had asked.

Judd Neep had. The elderly widow had showed up with some other old women the third or fourth night he had done his act. After the final prayer she had approached Judd, telling him that his message was a powerful one and that it proved God was always looking out for people who were in need. Gideon Cull had come over then and asked if she was in any special kind of need, and she had allowed that she was. She had been widowed for three years and

felt "so all alone," was the way she had put it. Cull had
sympathetically told her that surely she knew the Lord
was with her, to which she had responded that sometimes
she just was not sure.

Looking at the widow very intently with his deep-set
brown eyes, Cull had declared, "Mrs. Leffler, you will be
sure. I give you my promise. And I aim to make it my
mission that you will be sure. May I call upon you
tomorrow?"

She had said yes, and the preacher had called, continuing to do so just about every day for the next three
weeks. Judd had asked him once how the old mission was
getting on, but Cull had not taken kindly to the joke. In
fact, he had said nothing at all about the Widow Leffler
until the night before they had left Ehrenberg.

"She is very ill, Judd," Cull had announced in a sad
voice. "I expect she will die very soon. Tomorrow, on our
way out of town, I will visit her one last time. Perhaps, if
it is God's will, she will make a substantial donation to
further our work."

The next morning the young man had waited with the
horses outside Sarah Leffler's house. Cull had been inside
for only half an hour or so, and when he had emerged, his
face was stern, and he had stayed silent for the better part
of an hour as they rode. Then he had seemed to brighten.

"She was very kind to us, Judd," the preacher had
revealed. "In her last moments, she was very kind." Opening his Bible satchel, Cull had showed Judd the gold coins
and jewelry inside.

"She gave you all that?" Judd had exclaimed, astonished. When Cull had nodded, the young man had murmured, " 'Last moments,' you said. Is she . . . ?"

The preacher had nodded gravely. "Mrs. Leffler has
passed beyond the torments of this world to meet whatever everlasting future the Lord in His divine wisdom has
planned for her soul. That was her mission. Her mission
also, as it happens, was to materially assist us in carrying
out *our* mission."

They had continued with their mission in several small towns up and down the Arizona side of the Colorado River, and a pattern soon emerged—all involving elderly widows. In La Paz, there had been a Widow McNulty, who had also died on their last morning in town. And in Castle Dome, a very short time ago, there had been the Widow Anderson.

However, the circumstances that last time had been different—two ways different. First, Judd Neep had actually seen the woman after Gideon Cull had visited her. Second, the preacher had run out on his young cohort, apparently having decided it was time to carry on with his mission alone.

Shaking himself from his reverie, Judd Neep smiled to himself, thinking that if the mission of the Reverend Gideon Cull was to run, the mission of the young man he had deserted was to follow—even if he had to follow all the way to Tucson and beyond. Probably, though, he would catch up with the stagecoach long before Tucson, since it stopped for overnights along the way. Having two mounts to switch off with, however, enabled Judd to keep going.

A look of grim determination on his angular face, Judd told himself that he would get what he had coming . . . and so would Gideon Cull. Cull might think he had ended their partnership, but it was going to be Judd who ended it—with a bullet, maybe from his new fancy Winchester.

He stopped the horses and looked back at the adobe station. From that distance it looked like a small, lonely black dot—and inside was a dead old man who would never be lonely again.

Taking off his hat and wiping his sweating face, Judd Neep smiled his strangely humorless smile. That was the sort of thing the preacher would say. In fact, the young killer could now remember Cull saying almost that exact same thing about the Widow Anderson before she had died. It had been a day or so before Judd had gone to the woman's house, finding her smothered dead under her pillow and her money and jewels missing. Cull had taken them and had left his cohort to take the blame.

That ain't a fair way to divvy things up, Judd told himself as he spurred his horse after the stagecoach. *Not one bit fair.*

Chapter Three

The intense heat of the day seemed to double itself inside the coach as the stage rolled eastward. Isabel Hallan, Gideon Cull, and Lyman Whisters slept, the salesman snoring noisily but in almost perfect rhythm with the gentle swaying and dipping of the stage. Looking across at Rado Kane, Crystal Richmond could not determine whether he was asleep or not, what with his ever-present hat covering most of his face. He seemed completely relaxed, as one does in sleep; but then, the gunfighter seemed to be a man who could relax at will, with his waking state not seeming to differ much from a man lost to the world of slumber.

Holding aside the leather curtain, Crystal gazed at the surrounding countryside with complete awe. The land— the western reaches of the Sonora Desert, the peddler had told her—looked burned out, as if the great final fire or the great final desolation that was promised repeatedly in both the Old and New Testaments had already been carried out. "And I will make your cities waste. And I will bring the land unto desolation," was the Almighty's way of putting it in the Book of Leviticus.

She did not need to borrow a Good Book from the Reverend Cull's satchel to recall the words, but it was the preacher who, with his Bible-quoting and perhaps even by his very presence, had brought them back to her. She had managed over time to drive those fiery death-and-destruction scenes of rotting corpses and screaming multitudes from her conscious mind. Now and again one would still emerge from within the deepest of her dreams to haunt her, but it happened less and less frequently as the years passed. Now, seated on a stagecoach to Tucson, the memories of her terrified child-mind were back in full force.

She had been a girl of fifteen when her father had begun the descent into his personal mental and physical hell that ended in his suicide nine months later. It had been from a traveling evangelist that her father had first heard the message of doom that was to take hold of his life, and though she had never seen the preacher, she now wondered if he had resembled the Reverend Gideon Cull. Watching the preacher rocking peacefully in his seat across from her, Crystal could easily picture him in the role of a doomsday preacher.

She had not thought about her father for some time, driving from her mind his religious ravings, his fevered disdain of her mother and herself, and the moral outrage he particularly directed toward the life of singing and dancing his daughter had wanted so much.

"The satyrs, those bastard children of Satan, dance!" he had screamed at her. "So says Isaiah. And who are the adulterous temptresses of the righteous? Jezebel, Delilah, and Salome! And did they not also perform their whoresome dances in the cause of evil? Were they not evil incarnate themselves? And as they were, you wish to be?"

Blaming her mother for his daughter's erring ways, he had declared, "Have I not left the bringing up of my only child to a woman who was *supposed* to be managing my home, while I worked my fingers to the bone to put meat on our table?"

His scorn had encompassed the city of Chicago as well, which became identified in his tortured mind with Babylon—that harlot-infested capital of despicable sin all of God's prophets had been so bent on annihilating. Prophesying of the future in store for Chicago, he had predicted, "The kings of the earth, who have committed fornication and lived deliciously with her, shall bewail her and lament for her when they shall see the smoke of her burning." He no doubt had died disappointed when the city he had deemed a latter-day Babylon had not been visited by the Lord's wrath.

Crystal's mother, worn out by the nine-month-long ordeal, had died less than a year afterward. Luckily, Crystal's matron aunt Ruth had been agreeable to taking in the only child of her departed sister—and Aunt Ruth had had no preconceived notions about acting and dancing.

Sighing, Crystal wondered briefly if Gideon Cull, too, preached that all living things would be blasted to hell. Suddenly she smiled, thinking that perhaps the Lord had used the Sonora Desert to practice. If so, the earth had shown a certain measure of defiance, for through the shimmering heat of the noonday sun she could see a variety of plant life living in the seemingly unfertile sand.

No doubt her father would have said that they would be punished in time. Or perhaps they were being punished now. Perhaps the very struggle to remain alive was their eternal punishment. If so, perhaps the great final ending of all things was not something that would happen just once but was an event that would last for an eternity. It was not an impossible thought when one looked out on the Sonora Desert baking under a blistering sun.

Dropping the leather curtain, she turned her head straight ahead, her eyes taking a few moments to adjust from the brightness of the outside to the relatively dim light of the coach interior.

"Are you all right, Miss Richmond?"

She realized she was staring at Rado Kane. His hat was now off, and his penetrating pale eyes were directly on her own.

"Y-yes. I'm fine, thank you."

"You didn't look it, for a moment."

"The desert . . . the desolation . . . I guess I was just lost in my thoughts."

Nodding, he smiled with understanding. "It can do

that to you, the first time you see it. Farther east, it gets even more lonely." That said, he fell silent again.

A sudden shiver went down Crystal's spine, feeling like a cold finger contrasting with the heat. The desert in California had not affected her in the same way, and she was sure her current reaction was because of Gideon Cull, the memories of her father, and perhaps Rado Kane himself and what had happened in Yuma.

She tried to shake off the black feeling. Talking would help, even talking to the man who sat across the coach from her. Though she really had no interest in him, she had to admit that he might not be all that unattractive, properly dressed and cleaned up. In any case, clearly one had to do something with the time or go slowly out of one's mind.

Trying to engage Kane in conversation, she remarked, "The Indians fought so hard to keep this land. Why?"

Kane looked at her for a moment, then shrugged. "People fight to keep what they have—or to take what others have. Like other people, Indians fight for both reasons."

"And you, Mr. Kane, why do you fight?"

"I try not to, Miss Richmond."

"I find that hard to accept," she responded, with more skepticism in her voice than she had intended.

"If you're thinking about that boy—"

She shook her head. "Not just him. I mean, not just what happened. I suppose you could have killed him after he was down, and you didn't. But you—"

"What I did was take out his gun hand. I didn't much like the thought of him following after me," Kane said in a wry tone.

Shaking her head again, she countered, "But he wouldn't have challenged you at all if you weren't—What I mean to say is—"

"If I wasn't a gunfighter?"

"Yes. That's what you are, isn't it?"

Nodding, he confirmed, "I carry a gun, yes—more than one, actually—and I use guns to earn my living."

"Do you consider that an honorable profession?"

For an instant the ironic, crooked smile Crystal had learned to expect from the gunfighter formed on Kane's face. "You folks in all your Northern cities thought so when I did the same thing in your army. As I recall, the more people I killed, the more honorable I was."

"But that was different, Mr. Kane," Crystal objected, somewhat nervously smoothing the folds of her skirt. "That was war."

He shrugged again. "War or peace, killing is killing, and dead is just as dead. That's the first thing. The second is that if you look around real close, you'll find that the war's not exactly over with in some places out here."

Finding his attitude insufferable, she lifted her chin in indignation and retorted, "Other men fought in the war, Mr. Kane. But they now do different things . . . useful things."

"Maybe they weren't trained as well as I was. That's the only training I ever had, miss. Guns and using them. I learned well. Lots of men who didn't learn well didn't ever get the chance to think about what they might do afterward." Lifting the side curtain, he gestured outside with his chin, adding, "Anyway, a gun comes in handy out here."

Crystal shook her head. "A horrible place, your 'out here.' "

Peering intently at her with his probing eyes, he asked, "If San Francisco was all that great, why'd you leave?"

She answered quickly, "San Francisco was a dream—a shattered one."

"And Tucson? You think that'll be better?"

"If it's not"—she sighed—"there's always Chicago again." The very thought of returning to her home city, however, made her inwardly shudder. To return to Chicago would be to admit that she had failed, and while someday it might have to be considered, she would not do so now. She straightened in her seat and asked her fellow passenger, "This town that you're going to, your Gila Bend—what kind of place is that?"

"Not much of one. A saloon, a hotel, maybe a couple of other buildings. And Jack Sandeen."

"Who?"

"A man who I guess needs killing real bad," he answered softly.

"By you, Mr. Kane?" the young woman asked, her voice cold.

"No, not by me. My employer."

She looked at him quizzically. "Your employer?" she asked, unable to imagine someone hiring a gunfighter. "Who might that be?"

"A man named Angus Mallory. He owns a silver mine there. Apparently he's got a feud going with another mineowner, and *that* fellow has hired Sandeen—another professional gun hand—to run the town like he owned the place." Kane flashed another wry smile. "Apparently Mr. Mallory feels that a town ought to be available to be used by anybody who wants to. So he's hired me to even things out."

"And will you?" Crystal demanded. "Or will you just make things worse?"

Shrugging, Rado Kane pulled his hat back down over his eyes. "We'll see," he mumbled. "We'll see."

Seven miles northeast of Gila Bend, in an adobe building that served both as the office of Angus Mallory's mining operation and as living quarters for Mallory and his daughter, Katherine, the mood was tense. Six chairs ringed the wooden table in the center of the main room, five of them occupied by men sitting in stony silence. Only the tall young woman—her long blond hair swishing like a finely groomed horse's tail as she moved about the table serving coffee, and her blue eyes sparkling with anticipation —looked anything other than grim.

Katherine Mallory, who would be nineteen within the month, moved with the unstudied grace of someone at peace with herself, which belied the deep concern she had about the outcome of this meeting. So much depended on its success. She had tried many times before to make these men see reason and stop their wasteful hatred, but this time she *had* to be successful.

"Thank you, Katherine," her father said, looking at her with a mixture of affection and impatience as she placed a mug of coffee before him. Gripping the cup with his huge hands, Mallory sipped the coffee, then told his daughter gruffly, "You requested this meetin', so I agreed to it, but take your seat and let's get this thing started and over with." The blue eyes in his leathery face were cold as they regarded the three men seated opposite him—especially Seth and David Garlath, who were father and son, and their foreman, Clay Brock.

As Katherine sat in the chair between her father and Let Cutler, the foreman of the Mallory mine, she looked across at David Garlath and smiled. David was twenty-one, as dark as she was fair, and they had been in love since either of them could remember. *Please,* the young woman implored whatever destinies controlled their lives, *let there be some sanity here today.*

"All right, Mallory, start talking," Seth Garlath muttered as he dabbed with a bandanna at the perspiration gleaming on his balding head. "It's your meeting."

"It's Katherine's," Mallory replied, and his eyes, like his adversary's, were on her, waiting.

As different as they were alike, these two mineowners had shared much together, good times and bad, and now they shared so much enmity. Although both men were in their mid-fifties, physically they were opposites.

Angus Mallory was a big strapping man with bushy red hair surrounding his red, weatherbeaten face, and his hands were thick and almost as wide as a small spade. Seth Garlath, whose sparse hair was mostly gray, was smaller than Mallory in every respect. Yet his inner strength

had proven equal to the bigger man's in many ways—both
before and after their personal relationship had turned
bitter.

"It's Katherine's meetin'," Mallory repeated.

"And mine," David Garlath put in. "We want to talk
about our marriage."

Mallory scowled at the younger Garlath. "Then this
will be a very short talk," he snapped.

"Father!" Katherine declared, horrified that before
they had even begun, things were deteriorating.

Seth Garlath nodded. "That's one thing I'll agree
with, Katherine. There's no point in talking about this. If
you had any sense about you, you'd know that."

Let Cutler cleared his throat. "Look, if this is a family-
type discussion, there's no need for me and Brock to be
here." He gestured toward his counterpart sitting uneasily
between the two Garlaths.

"There's every reason," Katherine said. "If there's to
be peace between our two mining camps, you both need
to know about it—and enforce it."

"Peace." Garlath uttered the word as if his mouth
were full of lime.

"Please," Katherine implored, looking back and forth
between the two mineowners. "Once you were friends—
once you were much more than friends—and you would
have been delighted for David and me to officially bond
the Mallory and Garlath families . . . or what's left of
them."

Once. It sounded like the beginning of all those fairy
tales: Once upon a time. Once these two men had worked
side by side in firm partnership as they carved their living
from the crust of the earth mining gold and then silver
from the M&G mines—a succession of them, first in California and then in Nevada. The precious metals never
came in abundance, but they had amply provided the men
and their families the basics of food, clothing, and shelter

and also had provided for the well-being of a succession of small crews.

And then, ten years ago in Virginia City, Nevada, their lives had literally gone up in flames, when the wooden houses they had lived in burned. Waiting together as usual for their husbands to return home from their traditional Saturday night in town with their hired men, Glenna Mallory and Ellen Garlath had put their two children to bed in Katherine's bedroom—it was Glenna's turn to play hostess—and then the women had sat and sewed, talking quietly.

How the fire had started was never clear to Katherine. There was talk afterward of a kerosene lamp overturning or perhaps flames escaping from the cookstove that had provided all the heat there was after the sun went down. But Katherine's memory was very clear about her mother, her dress in flames, coming into her room screaming for Katherine and David to wake up and get out of there. She remembered the blanket being thrown over her and David as, screaming themselves, they had been pushed to the door through sheets of searing flames.

By the time the closest neighbors came to the scene, the fire had taken its toll. David's mother had been trapped within the building as its walls and roof of fire collapsed. Katherine's mother, having shepherded the children away from harm, had fallen unconscious. She had died two days later from the extensive burns all over her body. Her mother had been a beautiful woman, Katherine had thought as a child. She was no longer beautiful when she died.

Their joint tragedy had seemed to bring Mallory and Garlath even closer together as they continued to work the Nevada earth. And then, five years ago, the partners had decided to try their luck in the Arizona Territory, for stories of great silver lodes were many. The land was hard and the living harder, the stories had said, but for any man willing to pay the rigorous price, the Almighty had placed beneath that land a storehouse of precious metal three times bigger than what lay beneath California and more than twice what Nevada could boast.

It had gone badly from the beginning. Deciding to work two separate digs, neither partner had produced much for his effort—or so each claimed. Katherine could not recall which of them had first accused the other of cheating, but after that first accusation the bad blood had spread like a disease, poisoning their relationship and setting their workers against each other in brawls at the smallest provocation. Within a year the partnership had dissolved, leaving each with his half of the venture—and with the deep suspicion that the other had gotten the real lode.

Although Katherine and David had continually argued that no lode had been discovered and probably never would be, neither of their fathers would alter his stance.

"The silver is here," Angus Mallory had told her. "But the stories are true about the price to be paid for it—and Seth Garlath has paid the price. He's traded his honesty for greed. And while I don't feel the boy is basically dishonest, he *is* Garlath's son, after all. And blood is blood."

It had continued that way from then on, and what had once been was no longer—except for Katherine's love for David and his for her.

"David and I," she said now, alternately looking at her father and David's, "wish to do as you had once hoped: get married and unite our families. We also wish for your blessings. Despite your objections, we've continued to see each other, but we want this feud between you to end before we join our families in the eyes of God. You both—"

Seth Garlath abruptly stood up and put his hands on his hips. With his dark eyes narrowed, he angrily told Katherine, "I think I've heard just about enough. You talk of marriage, do you? You talk of joining our families?

Why? Have you discovered that your vein of silver heads in the direction of Garlath property?"

"What vein of silver?" Angus Mallory snorted, jumping up from the table as well.

"Yes, what vein?" David echoed. "Dad, we've got both foremen here. What do Cutler and Brock have to say?" He looked in turn at each of the men, who had been silent. "Well?" the young man demanded. "Just how much precious silver have you been digging out?"

Before either of the foremen could speak, Mallory laughed derisively, and his voice was mocking as he declared, "Nice try, boy! Naturally, you and Brock had yourselves a little rehearsal before comin' here."

Seth Garlath retorted, "Same could be said for your man." Addressing Katherine again, he muttered, "As to this marriage business, young lady, you can forget it."

David rose slowly. "Suppose *I* don't choose to forget it?"

"That would be a bad decision, son," Seth warned. "If you marry this Mallory girl, I don't want to see your face ever again. Now, let's get out of here."

"No, not yet," Katherine cried, her eyes beseeching. "There's something else David and I want to say."

"About marrying?" Garlath asked coldly.

She shook her head, and suddenly a hint of a smile was on her face. "Something else. David and I have a proposal for the two of you. Since neither of you will listen to reason, and both of you keep insisting the other's mine is the richer one, simply exchange mines. Trade one for the other."

Angus Mallory looked at his daughter as though she had lost her mind, then yelled, "*That* is your proposal?"

Snorting loudly, Seth Garlath countered, "I've got a proposal of my own, girl, one I've made to your father lots of times before: Sell me your digs. If there's no lode there, he ought to be willing enough."

Angus Mallory's arm shot out, his finger stabbing the air. "I've made you the same offer, Garlath—and you've refused. Don't think I don't know why. You know damned well where the silver is, you son of a—"

"Damn you!" Katherine shouted, rising so quickly that her chair crashed to the floor like a gunshot. Both foremen glanced at each other and rose slowly, edging out of the inner circle of the warring families. "Damn both of you!" the young woman exclaimed. In spite of herself, in spite of the lecture she had given herself to remain in total control, she could feel the tears welling up in her eyes. "Even if one of you were sitting right on top of a mother lode, how would you ever know? You're too busy fighting with one another!"

"And who started it, missy?" Seth Garlath demanded. "Who was it who first started his men attacking whose? Who, I want to know?"

"And who," Mallory countered, "when the fists in his hire couldn't match the fists in mine, hired himself a professional gun?"

Garlath glared at his former friend. "Sandeen is insurance, that's all he is. He hasn't shot anybody yet. Besides, I hear that the Mallory mining interests have sent for their own gun to come to Gila Bend."

Mallory wheeled toward his daughter, his face taut. "Katherine—"

"I told David about it, yes," she admitted, "because it's wrong."

"And Sandeen is right?"

"No," David interjected. "Sandeen should be paid off and sent away now. And your man, Mr. Mallory, should be told to stay on whatever stage is bringing him here— before things get really out of hand." The young man turned to his father. "You say nobody has been shot, but two nights ago Sandeen threatened two Mallory men in the saloon, saying that no Mallory workers were to be seen in town. He also said that was by your order."

"Nothing came of it," the elder Garlath said, shrugging. "Mallory's men were smart enough to move on."

Let Cutler suddenly moved toward the table. The

tall, muscular foreman eyed Seth Garlath and countered, "They were smart enough not to get themselves shot on the spot, is what you mean."

"Same thing," Garlath said evenly. "Think of it this way, Cutler. You Mallory boys come to town and start drinking, there could be trouble. This is just my way of keeping the peace." He smiled at Katherine and David. "You see? I believe in peace, just like you do."

"That won't do," Cutler insisted, his deeply tanned face flushing angrily. "You can't stake out the whole of Gila Bend as Garlath territory. My men need a place to drink and play cards, too."

Mallory raised a big red hand and pointed at Cutler. "You'll do your drinkin' and cards up here, Let. I'll get whiskey sent up from the saloon. That way you'll all stay out of Sandeen's way. And you'll all be here—just in case somebody gets the idea in his head to take the mine by force."

"The men won't like it," his foreman said.

"It won't be for long, Let." Mallory's eyes burned with inner rage as he stared into Seth Garlath's face. "I promise, it won't be for long."

"It won't be for long," Clay Brock, Seth Garlath's foreman, repeated as he stood in Gila Bend's only saloon later that evening. He rubbed his thick brown beard. "That's exactly how Mallory put it."

Brock downed the whiskey in one gulp and placed the empty glass on the table before him. It was immediately refilled by a black-gloved hand. The man across the table from Brock—the only other person in the saloon except for Hawk Brown, the owner—was dressed completely in black, from his well-shined boots to the black kerchief around his neck. "Black is fitting for certain occupations," Jack Sandeen had said once. "For undertakers, preachers, and the men who serve up the death that gives both of them a living." But Brock had figured black would have been a natural color for the gunfighter *without* any fancy explanation.

Black was also the color of the man's shoulder-length hair, which was combed straight back from his forehead and ears. The man's eyes were black, too—as black as dead coals of a fire long burned out. The only aspect of lightness about Jack Sandeen was his pale face, especially one jagged white line a knife blade had carved from below the left ear to a spot just above the left corner of Sandeen's mouth that gave him a permanent, sardonic smile. As the foreman regarded the man, he thought to himself that when Sandeen's eyes and smile were directed toward you, your guts churned and turned cold. At least they had that effect on Brock, and Clay Brock was a man who was not intimidated by anyone . . . usually.

For beyond the smile and eyes and clothes there was something else that was black about Sandeen that Brock and, he supposed, others felt. There was a black dead-liness—or perhaps a deadness—to the way he carried himself and even to the soft, whispering way the man talked. Brock had never heard the gunfighter speak louder than that rasping whisper, the one he was speaking in now, the one that was making Brock's hand shake as he lifted the second glass of whiskey to his lips.

"'It won't be long,'" Sandeen quoted. "He means Rado Kane."

"*His* gunfighter?"

Sandeen nodded. "That's right."

"Is he good?"

Flashing his sardonic smile, the gun hand answered, "He's still alive, and that says something. But the way I hear it, he's got himself a real weakness. He doesn't like to kill."

Brock shuddered. Not liking to kill was a weakness! The foreman hated this whole thing. He was a working man, not a fighting man. He had had his share of brawls, yes—you could not be a foreman for very long without being able to take care of yourself and now and then having to prove it. But even in the worst of fights, you only fought to protect yourself. Sure, killing could come as a result. In fact, Brock had once unintentionally killed a man with a chair in a saloon fight. But killing was never intentional among the men Brock knew. He was certain that he knew Seth Garlath fairly well, and even he would not want Angus Mallory killed, no matter what he might say about his ex-partner. And yet he had hired Jack Sandeen—a man who judged another man weak for not liking to kill.

"This Kane, he actually goes out of his way not to kill," the gunfighter went on as he poured the foreman a third drink. "Even men who call him out." He smiled cruelly, declaring, "Well, now, let's lift our glasses to Mallory's gunfighter, Rado Kane," Sandeen whispered, "and to his very fatal weakness."

Chapter Four

It was late afternoon, and Crystal Richmond nearly jumped out of her skin as the leather curtain beside Rado Kane suddenly parted. Bright sunlight streamed in for a few seconds, then the window was filled with the face of Sam Loomis.

"Don't mean to cause anybody undue alarm," the shotgunner said, "but it would be a good idea if you all had your weapons ready. We got us some company." With that he was gone, the leather curtain back in place.

"Company?" Crystal asked, puzzled.

Isabel Hallan finally removed her hat from her face. "The trouble has come," she declared matter-of-factly to no one in particular.

Lyman Whisters shook himself awake, then prodded the preacher. "You got anything we can use in that bag of yours?" he queried.

Gideon Cull looked both alarmed and confused. "What . . . what do you mean?"

"He means a gun, Reverend," Kane answered. "One of these." Kane held up his revolver, checking the load. He then nodded at Whisters, asking, "And how about you?"

"I trust this will suffice," the peddler replied, pulling a long-barreled Army Colt from his checkered canvas bag. "It's not the latest model, but it's been useful to me in the past."

"Well, Reverend?" Kane asked again. "You carrying any weapons in that bag of yours?"

"A gun? Why?"

Kane pulled back the leather curtain to his right and tied it in place. Gesturing outside with his chin, he growled, "That's why."

Whisters had tied back the other curtain, giving the passengers a view of the terrain on either side of the coach. Craning their necks, the passengers could see a large group of men on horseback lined up in a ragged semicircle farther ahead on the road, looking like little more than miniature statues from that distance. There could be little doubt what they were waiting for.

"One of the few nice things about the desert," Whisters remarked, "is that it's very hard to ambush anybody out here. No place to hide." He checked the cylinder of his pistol and nodded in satisfaction that it carried the correct consignment of six bullets.

"That disadvantage also applies to the target," Kane pointed out. "Here," he said to Crystal, extending Billy Nathan's pistol to her, handle first. "This time I won't take no for an answer. Mr. Whisters, show her what she needs to know—right quick, if you please."

"Who are they?" Cull asked as he stared out the window. His left hand was still clutching his black bag to his chest, but his right one was now filled with a short-barreled pistol.

Again Sam Loomis's face appeared in the window beside Kane. He looked at the weapons that the passengers had armed themselves with, then said, "Them little guns might be okay if they get real close, but I'm hopin' we can see to it they don't. I got a couple of rifles for two of you folks—if you'll oblige, Mr. Whisters and Reverend Cull." He then addressed the gunfighter. "Mr. Kane, I could use you on top, if you'll be so kind. The view's much better from up here." Then his face once again disappeared as he hauled himself back up.

"Who are they?" Cull asked again.

"They look to be wearing sombreros," Whisters answered. "Probably them Mexicans, after the payroll."

"But I thought this transport wasn't carrying any payroll!" Cull protested.

Whisters nodded, smiling wryly. "We're not. But if you like, we can stop so's you can explain that to them, Preacher. They might even believe you, you being a man of the Book and all."

Kane opened the coach door and stepped into the doorway, reaching up. The top half of his body momentarily disappeared from view, and then his left hand was back, two rifles in it. "Here, Whisters. These are for you and the Reverend," he announced.

"What about me?" Mrs. Hallan asked, clearly disappointed. "Where's a gun for me? I'm not as helpless as I may look to some."

"One second, ma'am," Kane's disembodied voice responded. He called out to Loomis, and after a short space of time he bent down and handed the woman one of Loomis's Navy Colts. Watching her carefully as she broke the pistol open, checked it, and snapped it shut, he then smiled and told her, "You don't look at all helpless to me, ma'am."

"Thank you, young man," she said, giving the cylinder a spin.

The gunfighter then looked at Crystal. "And you, Miss Richmond, you stay with that pistol I gave you—and use it."

"I—I don't think I can," she protested.

Kane abruptly pulled himself back inside the coach. Hovering over the young woman, he said stiffly, "Miss Richmond, I respect a person's right not to like anything they choose not to like, and that includes guns. But this is a little different. You ever see a carnival shooting gallery, where you shoot at moving ducks?"

"Well, yes, but—"

"Keep that carnival picture in your mind and understand this: Right now you're one of the ducks. Now, those

ducks' odds are pretty bad unless somebody gets the shoot-
ers to stop, and right now, nobody's around to get that
done for us—except us ducks."

Crystal stared at the heavy pistol clutched in both her
hands. "I've never fired a gun before," she said softly.

"The Lord will protect his own," Gideon Cull promised, snatching up a rifle and cocking it.

Turning to the older woman on his left, Whisters
peered intently at her face and asked, "Will He, Mrs.
Hallan? Will the Lord be protecting us?"

She regarded him blankly.

"You knew something was going to happen," the peddler remarked, his voice tight. "'The trouble has come,'
that's what you said. Well, it surely has, ma'am, and I'm
just wondering if you know how it'll turn out."

Her eyes narrowed. Indicating the preacher, Mrs.
Hallan declared, "As for the Lord, I believe He protects
those who do something to protect themselves." Smiling
knowingly at the salesman, she added, "Therefore I suggest you see to your weapon, Mr. Whisters—or things will
turn out very badly."

After giving each of the passengers a quick glance,
Rado Kane stepped back outside and pulled himself up to
the box.

"Welcome to the top," Walt Grader declared as Kane
seated himself between the driver and the shotgun guard.
"I was gonna invite you up anyway, but now's better than
later."

"I'm honored," Kane said, grinning crookedly. He
had traveled enough stagecoaches to know that an invita-
tion from the driver to ride on top was a real individual
courtesy—at least when the weather was right. And the
weather at the moment was just fine.

"Here, take this," Sam Loomis ordered, handing Kane
a Winchester. "I hope you can handle it as well as you do
a pistol."

Grabbing hold of the rifle, Kane remarked, "You've
got yourself a regular arsenal on this coach."

"Well, I don't know if it's exactly regular," Loomis quipped, "but it increases my personal comfort some. How're the folks below?"

"A mite nervous."

Nodding, the shotgun guard pointed out, "They'd be stupid if they weren't. Can any of them shoot?"

"Three of them sure will be trying," Kane assured him.

"So will they," Loomis retorted, sweeping his rifle barrel in an arc toward the men arrayed down the road in front of them.

Kane tightened the leather thong under his chin that held his hat in place. From under the brim his eyes slowly scanned the late afternoon horizon before them. He now counted more than twenty horsemen, and Whisters had been right about the hats. There was no mistaking them now. They were Mexican sombreros, all right. "I don't make out any rifles," the gunfighter observed.

"Me neither," Loomis agreed. "But that don't say they don't have 'em, just that they're not showin' 'em yet. No need to, at least for a few minutes. *We're* coming to *them*—so they can afford to be patient."

"You been attacked before like this?" Kane asked.

"A couple of times. Once with Walt here."

Grader nodded, but his eyes stayed straight ahead. The driver held the reins steady in his left hand, while his right hand hovered close to a short-barreled Winchester carbine cradled in his lap. Kane noticed that the speed of the coach had neither slowed nor increased since the spotting of the Mexicans.

As if reading his mind, Loomis said, "When we're within easier rifle range, Walt'll give the team its full head. Hang on, because the ride'll get rocky. When you start shootin', aim for anybody in front of us, 'cause they'll be tryin' to hit the horses."

"What about the others?"

Loomis flashed an ironic grin. "They'll be tryin' for *us*."

A single gunshot punctuated his statement.

"Somebody just ran out of patience," Grader growled, and then the rain of lead began.

The reins snapped in Grader's hands, and the stage lurched as if the coach, horses and all, had been blown from a cannon. The line of horsemen up ahead was suddenly a lot closer than it had been and getting closer at the gallop, and the Mexicans started charging the stage even as it charged at them, their semicircle closing like the jaws of some large desert lizard.

"In front!" Loomis shouted. "The ones in—"

A bullet ricocheted off the luggage rack behind Kane, and the loud metallic *twang* cut off the end of Loomis's statement, but the gunfighter got the message. He swung his Winchester's sights on the oncoming rider directly in front of the horses ahead and squeezed the trigger. The man who had been in the gunsights was jerked from his saddle as if he had had a hangman's noose around his neck.

Loomis's Henry boomed twice in rapid succession, and suddenly another horse ahead was riderless. "Damn!" he shouted. "Missed the other son of a—"

Kane's rifle sounded again, cutting off Loomis's word, and then a third Mexican, to the front and left, was flat on the sand. Just then a bullet whistled past Kane's right ear, and he jerked his head in that direction.

"Sons of the Abomination!" came a cry from within the coach. "Oh, Lord, hear me! Like Thy servant Jeremiah, I implore Thee to let me see Thy vengeance pour upon these blasphemous vermin who praise and do honor to the beast Satan! And as Thou promised Thy faithful prophet Isaiah, avenge Ye now of Thine enemies, these heathen swine who come upon us in stealth and seek to—"

"Dammit, Reverend!" came Lyman Whisters's unmistakable voice. "Will you kindly shut your flapping mouth and try to shoot some of those heathen swine instead of talking them to death?"

As if in swift obedience on its own, the rifle barrel

that was half extended from the coach's far window fired,
and a horse off to the right bucked its rider and then
crashed to the earth. "The Lord in Heaven be praised!"
the Reverend Gideon Cull crowed in jubilation.

"*In front!*" Sam Loomis shouted. "*We're going through!*"

Rado Kane's head whipped back around, and his eyes
blinked in surprise to see the Mexicans very much closer
now. They were so close that he could see the colors of
their sombrero bands.

Loomis's rifle cracked off three fast shots, dropping
two of the bandits. As Kane squeezed off two slugs—one
hitting its target—he snapped up his sawed-off shotgun.
"*Duck!*" he yelled. Kane and Grader both ducked, just as
Loomis pushed the business end of the gun behind the
driver and let a blast fly at two riders coming at them.
Both horses reared back at the impact of the pellets, but
what happened to their riders Kane could not see, as they
were down and out of his range of vision in a flash.

"We're through them!" Loomis shouted triumphantly.
"Now *keep* them back!"

Turning to his left, Kane immediately rested his elbow on the wooden roof and brought his eye down to the
gunsight. He squeezed off another round, and another
Mexican left his horse. Then, from the corner of his eye,
he saw a rider taking careful aim at the driver's box. Kane
fired two rapid, badly aimed shots, and one of them hit
nothing; the other caught the bandit in the leg, but not
before his gun fired.

"*Damn!*" Loomis yelled.

"You hit?" Kane shouted over his shoulder.

"Nothin' but a bee sting," the shotgunner called back.
Laughing, he added, "Well, maybe a scorpion. Keep
shootin'!"

A pistol fired from the far side of the coach, and one
bandit's horse stumbled and went down on top of its rider.
Kane wondered whether the shot had been fired by the
young woman, but then he heard Whisters shout gleefully, "Good one, Mrs. Hallan!"

Gideon Cull's rifle sang out, but he missed his target. He groaned loudly, then called out, "Lord, I beseech Thee! Help Thine innocent servants who do Thy service, who pledge eternally ever to do Thy—"

"*Reverend!*" Whisters shouted. "Will the Lord's servant be ever so kind, I beseech *thee* once again, as to *shut the hell up!*"

Both Kane and Loomis were lying on their stomachs on the top of the coach, facing toward the rear. Behind the stage the bandits were thundering after them in four ragged columns five to ten yards apart, each with three or four riders with revolvers blazing.

"Reloadin'!" Loomis declared as he pushed himself back and extracted a box of shells for his Henry from under the seat. "Here's a box for you, Kane!" he added, slapping another to the left of the gunfighter's elbow. When Kane looked over, he saw the shotgun guard's shirt was soaked with blood at the right shoulder. He also saw Loomis wince with pain as he shoved the cartridges home.

A slug abruptly splintered the low wooden rail grip to Kane's right, telling him he was looking in the wrong direction, and he immediately aimed his rifle toward one of the four columns that were keeping pace with the stage. His heart pounding rapidly, he realized that the outlaws were bit by bit closing the distance.

Kane squeezed off a round, missed, then squeezed the trigger of the Winchester again. It clicked on empty.

"I'm out of shells!" Whisters called from below.

"Use your pistols," Kane yelled back, drawing his own Colt from its holster.

A rifle crack came from Cull's side of the coach, and a rider dropped. "Hosanna! Praise the Lord! Praise—"

The rest of the sentence was drowned in a fusillade of gunfire. Kane immediately lay as flat as he could, pressing his face against the roof of the stage. When the hail of bullets lessened, he looked up and saw that the lead riders in the two central columns had drastically closed the gap and were now very near the boot of the coach. Both hung low and close to the sides of their horses, a trick learned from the Indians, making them difficult targets. In spite of himself Kane appreciated the riding ability—but he did not appreciate its purpose.

"Boarders!" he shouted to Loomis.

"I see 'em!" the shotgun guard yelled back. His Henry exploded at Kane's left, and the rider closing in on Kane's right dropped to the ground—or at least part of him did. With his boot caught in his stirrup, he was dragged and bumped in a frenzied half circle that sent both central columns of riders in a disarrayed scramble to keep from colliding with their own members.

"Took care of that one real good!" Loomis crowed.

Kane barely heard the shotgunner, for he had his sights on the other rider, who was now coming in with lightning speed. *Got you,* Kane thought to himself, squeezing the trigger of his Colt. But just as he did, the stage jolted upward, and the bullet sailed far above his target. Realigning his gunsight, Kane found that the bandit was out of his line of vision.

"Where'd he go?" Kane yelled to Loomis.

"On the back! My side," Loomis shouted back. "I can't get there!"

Swiveling his head, Kane took a quick look at Loomis's pain-contorted face, then made a decision. In as fluid a motion as the rocking stage allowed, he lifted himself up, reached over and gripped the top railing with his left hand, then swung his legs over the side of the coach. The stage lurched again, and his body slammed into the door. He looked through the doorway, but his view of the opposite window was blocked by Lyman Whisters and Gideon Cull. *"Get down!"* he shouted at them, and they immediately ducked. His vision no longer blocked, what he saw at the window was the dirt-encrusted face of a Mexican—as well as a pistol barrel aimed directly at his own face.

"Buenos días!" the bandit said with a grin.

"Adiós!" Kane retorted, snapping up his Colt and

aiming it at the opposite window. His shot exploded into the face of the Mexican, who suddenly was gone from the window.

Then another shot exploded—this one from within the coach. A bullet whined past Kane's left ear, and his hat jerked backward, the thong around his neck cutting off his breath for a single surprising heartbeat. He squinted into the darkened coach interior.

"Oh, God! I-I'm sorry," Crystal Richmond blurted. Billy Nathan's smoking Colt was clutched in her two shaking hands. "God, I thought—"

"Damn!" the gunfighter exhaled. And then a bullet whizzed just beside the rail where his left hand still gripped. Pushing outward with his gun hand and kicking with both legs, he spun around, his back slamming into the coach side.

Two bandits were coming at him, and one of them was raising his revolver to shoot. Reacting immediately, Kane thumbed back the hammer and shot twice from the hip. Both riders went down.

Three rapid shots then sounded from over his head. Glancing up, he saw the business end of Loomis's rifle covering him.

"Nice shootin', son!" the shotgunner exclaimed. "Now, see if you can climb back up here—where it's safe."

Kane scrambled to the top of the coach, and as he did so, he once again thumbed back the hammer on the Colt.

"Easy, son, easy," Loomis suggested. "I think maybe they've decided that they took enough punishment for one day." Gesturing behind the coach with his chin, the weathered shotgunner asked with a wry smile, "What do *you* think?"

Kane looked back. The stagecoach was no longer being chased, and the bandits were reining in their horses. Counting rapidly, the gunfighter tallied eight Mexican riders remaining in their saddles, a few more chasing their mounts, and the rest of the band scattered along the stage road, either wounded or dead.

"I think," Kane remarked dryly, "I'll reload these guns."

Loomis made a sound that was half laugh, half groan.

"How bad you hit, Sam?" Walt Grader queried as he slowed the horses to a less frenzied pace.

"I've had worse. Bullet went clear through." Loomis grimaced, adding, "It made a helluva mess, though." He looked at Kane, nodding toward the gunfighter's hat. "You seem to have been lucky, too. From the looks of that bullet hole, one of them almost took your head off."

Loosening the thong under his chin, Rado Kane pulled off the black plainsman's hat and frowned as he examined the still-smoldering bullet hole in the left side of the brim.

"Lucky is right," he grumbled. "But it wasn't one of them, it was one of us." He shook his head. "At the very first opportunity, I'm gonna give that little lady some shooting lessons—whether she wants 'em or not."

Chapter Five

"**Y**ep, we sure are lucky!" Let Cutler declared. The foreman smiled broadly at Angus and Katherine Mallory and continued, "We weren't planning on digging in that direction at all, but one of the crewmen got his instructions wrong." He barked out a laugh, adding, "To think, we got lucky because one of our workers is incompetent!"

Katherine hugged her father so hard that she nearly pulled him from his chair. "And to think as well," she remarked, "that this same room that had held so much gloom earlier today is now filled with so much promise."

Nodding, her father agreed. "A strike'll do that." Mallory pried his daughter's arms from around his neck, then asked his foreman, "Can you tell yet just how big it *is*, Let?"

"I won't go calling it a mother lode, but it appears it'll be a lot bigger than anything this mine has ever seen. It's a thick spur that looks to be heading due east."

The grin faded immediately from Angus Mallory's face. "Due east," he repeated, scowling. "Straight toward Garlath's diggin's. Damn! I knew he'd struck it!"

"Father!" Katherine cried out.

Cutler argued, "That isn't necessarily so, Mr. Mallory, since we got no way of knowing how far it extends. Like I said—"

Mallory banged his tin coffee cup onto the tabletop, spilling half its contents, and his eyes turned cold. "I got *every* way of knowin', 'cause I know Seth Garlath! I've known the man too many years not to know when he's dealin' his cards from the bottom of the deck!"

"But Father—" Katherine protested, and her blue eyes, which had been sparkling with pleasure moments before, suddenly filled with trepidation.

"And you, my girl, are not to breathe a word of this to David," her father warned her. "What David knows, Seth Garlath knows. And in my book, blood is blood." He turned to his foreman. "Let, you better be sure the men understand that this find is to be kept secret."

The foreman nodded. "They understand, but I'll tell 'em again."

"It's vitally important," the older man persisted. "If Garlath finds out what we've got, it might push him to move on us now . . . and that'll be too soon. If Rado Kane is on tomorrow's stage like he should be, we'll get things settled proper right soon."

Katherine slammed her own cup down, her blue eyes flashing. "I can't believe what I'm hearing!" she shouted, her temper winning out over her anguish. "Here you are, just after getting what is undoubtedly the best piece of news you've had in years, and in less than a blink of an eye you turn it into fuel to feed your hatred. You see the depth of this poison you and Seth Garlath have created? You should be jumping up and down with happiness! You should be celebrating!"

Mallory stood, his face redder than normal. "Young miss, I don't much like gettin' a lecture from my daughter, and I especially don't much like it in front of my foreman —or anybody else, for that matter. That said, girl, I agree with you bein' right about one thing: We should have us a celebration. And we'll do so just as soon as O'Rourke and Clancy get back here with the whiskey. I sent them out for it as soon as I heard the good news."

"Back?" Katherine questioned, worry creasing her pretty face. "Back from Gila Bend?"

"Where else do they have a saloon, and where else but a saloon do they have whiskey?"

"But Seth Garlath said—"

"He said for me and the men to stay out of town," Mallory finished. "Lord knows I don't like being told what to do by the likes of Seth Garlath, but I'm plannin' to do just that until Kane shows up. In the meantime, though, we ain't gonna go dry around here. Especially now that, like you say, we got us somethin' to celebrate."

"Don't worry, Miss Katherine," Cutler said. "O'Rourke and Clancy ain't troublemakers. They'll be in and out of Gila Bend and that saloon right quick. That's their orders."

Four of the eight small round tables in the Gila Bend saloon were occupied. Three men were playing poker at one of the tables, at two of the others pairs of men drank beer in silence, and Jack Sandeen sipped whiskey and dealt himself hands of solitaire at the fourth. No one was at the long bar except Hawk Brown, who stood behind it, wiping the top.

A rather short, thin man who owed his nickname to the large, beaklike nose that dominated his face, Hawk owned the saloon and also was serving as town marshal on a temporary basis. His notion of temporary was that he was happy to accept the additional duties with its meager salary until any real trouble cropped up that the shotgun behind his bar could not handle—such as the kind of trouble that would occur if Mallory's hired gunfighter really did show up on tomorrow's stage.

At the moment things were peaceful enough for Hawk to retain his so-called office, for everybody in the place worked for Seth Garlath. But *peaceful* was, after all, a relative word, for no place was really peaceful when you had a shooter in town—especially one like Jack Sandeen.

Hawk had seen gunfighters before, both in Gila Bend and in other places, but Sandeen was different. Hawk had never before looked in a man's eyes and felt his own mouth turn as dry as the desert sand. When the man in black spoke, even for something as innocuous as ordering a fresh bottle of whiskey, it was as though Death himself were speaking. The way Hawk saw it, you could probably classify men into two groups: killers and nonkillers. But the barkeep then made subcategories of the killers: Jack Sandeen and everybody else. There was no doubt in Hawk's mind that Sandeen was one of a kind. *Thank God*, he added to himself as he watched the man surreptitiously.

Turning his mind to Rado Kane, Hawk concluded that if he really was coming to Gila Bend, he was already dead. And if the barman played his cards right and managed not to be in a position where, by rights, he should try to stop the fight, things would be over quickly—and he would not have to take a leave from his temporary marshaling job. With Kane come and, as it were, gone fast, there would be peace once more in Gila Bend.

Already celebrating in his mind the successful conclusion of the incident, Hawk reached for a bottle of his own special reserve. That reminded him that Lyman Whisters ought to be coming through soon; in fact, the liquor peddler was overdue. He did not have much to offer that Hawk wanted or needed—Hawk had no call for those sweet French after-dinner liqueurs—but Whisters did occasionally manage to get hold of some of the whiskey they drank over in Scotland.

The barkeep had thought it strange to the taste at first, but he had grown to really like it. He was careful, though, not to let anybody else know about it, since Whisters never had many bottles. As soon as possible after acquiring Scottish whiskey, he repoured it into older, unlabeled bottles that he kept mixed in with his normal rotgut. The only thing that distinguished his special bottles from the regular ones was a small letter X he had thumbnailed into the top of the corks. *X marks the Scot*, he had thought, laughing to himself, thinking it a damned shame that his joke was one he could not share with anybody. Maybe he would tell Lyman Whisters when he came through next—but then again, maybe not. The peddler might not appreciate Hawk's hiding the stuff from his clientele.

He was pouring himself a measure from one of the X-marked bottles when Tom Clancy and Ed O'Rourke, two Mallory crewmen, entered the bar. He stopped what he was doing, lifted the half-filled glass of amber-colored liquid, and drained it, then immediately poured himself another. Celebrations of peace were not the only time a good stiff jolt was called for. *Damn!* Hawk exclaimed to himself. *Why couldn't the Mallory people have done what they'd been told?*

Clancy and O'Rourke stood by the batwing doors just long enough to accustom their eyes to the relative darkness of the interior of the saloon. Then they moved directly to the bar.

"Afternoon, Hawk," Clancy said, his voice low.

Hawk downed his second whiskey. "You aren't supposed to be in here," the barkeep advised the man coldly.

"We ain't plannin' on bein' here long," the workman assured him. "The boss sent us in for a dozen bottles of your finest. "We get that, you get your money, and we're on our way."

"Which won't be any too soon for us," O'Rourke added with emphasis.

Hawk studied the two men. Both were well into their thirties, perhaps even beyond the forty point, although it was hard to tell. Their faces and bodies showed the wear of years of toiling in other people's digs—and probably in a couple of their own as well—as they chased the siren call of fortunes hidden beneath the earth's crust, first to California or Nevada, and then, as the easy plays there panned out, back east to the Arizona Territory, which was starting to boast of lodes bigger than those in the far West. Some few of the seekers of gold and silver would make the big strike, but most of them would wind up dying early, either from hard work, hard living, or hard whiskey.

Glancing over O'Rourke's shoulder at the other miners seated in the saloon, Hawk decided there was no discernible difference between them and the Mallory men. If they had not been originally stamped from the same mold, years and years of grubbing precious metals from holes in the ground had shaped them into similarity. No, there was no difference between them at all—with two exceptions. The Mallory men were not supposed to be here, and they were wearing sidearms.

"A dozen bottles," Tom Clancy repeated as he transferred a small stack of coins from his vest pocket to the top of the bar.

"Right," Hawk said. But as he started to turn to the bar, the sharp sound from across the room of a chair scraping backward stopped him cold. The barkeep knew precisely where the sound had come from, and when he faced back around, Jack Sandeen was standing, his hands on his hips, and glowering at Clancy and O'Rourke.

"Well, well, what have we here?" came the gunfighter's rasping voice.

Neither Mallory man moved as they looked across the bar at Hawk, seemingly frozen to where they stood. Hawk swiftly turned to his shelves, and his hands made three quick trips from shelf to bartop, moving four bottles each time. On the final trip his hands were shaking so badly that they almost lost their load. His fingers still were trembling as he swept the coins from the bar to his pocket without counting them.

"Take your whiskey and go. Now," he advised the crewmen tersely.

Before the Mallory men had a chance to touch the bottles, Sandeen spoke again. "I'm talking to you two. Turning your back on somebody talking to you is a sign of real disrespect. A real serious disrespect."

Both men turned slowly.

"We ain't lookin' for no trouble," O'Rourke said quickly, sweat suddenly beading on his forehead and his clean-shaven upper lip.

Sandeen's scarred smile broadened. "Well, it sure does appear that you got yourself some anyway, don't it?

Mr. Garlath gave strict orders for you Mallory scum to stay outta here."

"We're gettin' out," Clancy promised.

His hands still shaking, Hawk pointed out, "That's right. They're leavin' right now, Mr. Sandeen."

Sandeen's eyes narrowed. "You takin' a hand in this, Hawk?"

"I—I don't see that there's anything to take a hand *in*, Mr. Sandeen," the barkeep stammered nervously.

"You don't, eh?" the gunfighter snapped. "Well, I see things a little different. And maybe you'd better move down the bar a mite, Hawk, 'cause where you are at present puts you in the line of fire." Sandeen's eyes narrowed dangerously as he added, "And leave that shotgun of yours where it's at."

After considering what Sandeen had said for a moment at most, Hawk moved along the bar to his right. Gila Bend was temporarily without a temporary marshal.

All eyes in the saloon were on the gunfighter as he moved around to the front of his table and stood watching the two Mallory workers. Sandeen was less than a dozen feet from the bar, rocking gently from foot to foot as he pulled snug the black glove on his right hand—his gun hand. "Well? What do you have to say for yourselves?" he finally demanded.

"Nothin', Sandeen," Tom Clancy mumbled. "We got the whiskey we paid for, so we're leavin' now."

"Leavin', are you? I'm afraid you men have missed the point. Goin' out of here ain't the point. Your comin' *in* here, *that* is the point. Or are you both too stupid to see that?"

O'Rourke shook his head, his jaw set angrily. "We got no quarrel with you, Sandeen. And what's between Garlath and Mallory is between them. We ain't part of any of it. We just work the mine."

"I might believe that . . . except that both of you are carryin' revolvers. Now, just what do mine workers need with guns?"

Clancy started to say something, but O'Rourke sharply elbowed him. "We're carryin' whiskey," he stated. "Somebody might get the idea to take it from us. The guns are for protection."

"In that case," Sandeen rasped, "I suggest you think about protectin' yourself right now—unless you two pieces of Irish baggage don't have the guts."

"Now, hold on! We ain't professional guns," O'Rourke protested.

"You ain't nothin', neither of you," Sandeen scoffed. "You're two pieces of Mick trash who don't have the manhood necessary to take a leak standin' up."

Clancy went rigid. "Listen, you son of a—"

"Shut up, Tom!" O'Rourke warned. Then he again addressed Sandeen. "Like I said, neither of us is a professional gun. Your boss said we wasn't to drink here, and we're not breakin' that rule. We don't think he's got any right to make it, but our boss says for us to abide by it, so we are. All we're doin' is gettin' whiskey for us to bring back and drink at our own digs. There was no rule set about that."

"The rule, dung heap, was that you stay outta this place altogether. You chose to ignore that rule, thereby ignorin' my employer, thereby ignorin' *me*. I don't like that. I also don't like either of you sons of booze-bellied Irish whores."

"Goddamn you!" Clancy roared. He took a swift step forward, brandishing his fists. "I'll show you who—"

The roar from Sandeen's gun brought every seated man to his feet, and they watched in stunned silence as the slug slammed dead center into Tom Clancy's heart. His back hit the bar, and then his head did the same as he slid to the floor.

"A hostile act," Sandeen muttered, holstering his smoking revolver. He looked at the men standing around him. "Definitely a hostile act. I believe everyone here saw the man go for his weapon?"

No one said a word. All eyes were on the dead Mallory worker.

"I'll ask my question again," Sandeen growled loudly. "Didn't this bastard go for his gun?"

Several of the Garlath men nodded, although the nods were barely perceptible, and their faces were grim.

"Hawk, how about you?" Sandeen asked.

Hawk shook his head. "I—I couldn't really see nothin' from back here, Mr. Sandeen. But . . . but if all these men say Clancy went for his gun, I—I guess I'll have to take their word for it."

Turning to Ed O'Rourke, Sandeen grinned maliciously. "You see how it is. Now, I think your former friend will nicely get across my message to Mallory, so haul him out of here—but leave the whiskey. I'll graciously accept it as payment of the fine for breakin' my rules. Unless, of course, you intend to use your gun for the purpose you say you brought it—to make sure the whiskey gets back to your digs?"

Hawk stepped back to the bar, shaken. "One death is enough!" he proclaimed. "O'Rourke, do you hear me?"

The miner pivoted and glared at the barkeep. His eyes filled with disgust, he answered, "I hear you, *Marshal*." Kneeling, he hoisted Clancy's body over his broad shoulders and stood. He then looked at the gunfighter and mocked, "You're a real brave man, Sandeen. All of you, you're all real brave men."

Sandeen merely laughed. "You be sure to tell your boss that every worker he sends to Gila Bend will have to walk his way through Jack Sandeen to get back alive. That includes Mallory himself *and* his gunfighter, Mr. Rado Kane."

The stagecoach arrived at Mohawk Station, one of the larger way stations on the route, as night was coming on. Here the employees and passengers would have supper, rest overnight, and depart in the morning after a hearty breakfast. Grateful for the opportunity to stretch and allow their bodies respite from the rolling and rocking they had endured during the day—and anticipating the pleasure of a restful night ahead—the guests at Mohawk were generally a happy lot. But to the stationmaster, Moses Elkins, and his wife, Sally, this particular set of guests seemed happier than most, and the reason was obvious to them both. It was not every day that an incoming stage had fought its way through a band of outlaws and won.

"You should've seen Kane in action, Moses!" Sam Loomis shouted from his end of the long table in the center of the large common room. The shotgun guard, Rado Kane, Walt Grader, Isabel Hallan, and Reverend Gideon Cull were already digging into the supper of beans and tortillas, not bothering to wait for Lyman Whisters, who was still outside, carefully and methodically checking his stock, and Crystal Richmond, who was freshening up.

Loomis was wearing a fresh shirt, under which was a bandage that had been carefully applied by Sally Elkins after she had cleaned the wound. The damage to the shotgunner was slight—or so he insisted. He also insisted on continuing the run.

"Moses," he now repeated, his eyes sparkling with glee, "you really should've seen Kane hangin' from that coach door and gunnin' them bandits right outta their saddles. You should've been there to see it!"

Sally laughed as she set a fresh pot of coffee on the table. "He should've been right where he was, Sam. I give him enough excitement right here."

After laughing loudly, Loomis remarked with a broad grin, "I'll bet you do, at that."

Kane nodded in agreement as he studied the woman, deciding that the lady probably was right. He guessed that the sturdy Mrs. Elkins was in her late forties. Her short body was thick, but he would not have called her fat, and her brown hair, piled up in a no-nonsense bun, showed flecks of gray. While her face was far from beautiful—not even pretty, really—there were many things written there: warmth, happiness, strength . . . and something more.

This was a woman who was content with her life; this also was a woman who loved her man.

Moses Elkins hardly looked to be the sort of man who could inspire that kind of love. In his early fifties and bald except for a black wisp of hair he tried to keep plastered down on the top of his head, Moses had a long narrow face that looked like nothing so much as that of a friendly dog. It was a rather soft face, in contrast to his work-hardened body, and it, too, was the face of a man genuinely content with life, and who deeply loved his woman.

"You been here long?" Kane asked the stationmaster as Elkins placed a second stack of tortillas on the table.

"Close to four years. Why?"

"Just wondered about the name."

"Moses?"

Kane shook his head. "Mohawk Station. The Mohawks were a tribe from way back East, the way I remember hearing it in school."

"You're right about that," Whisters answered from across the room as he stepped through the doorway. Hurrying to the table and sitting down, he reached for the tortillas and continued, "The tribe was from upper New York, before the Revolution."

Shaking his head, Kane asked, "Then why is a way station in Arizona named Mohawk?" He looked at Whisters, then at Moses Elkins.

"Never thought to ask," the stationmaster answered with a shrug.

Whisters swallowed a mouthful of tortilla. "Got a theory?"

"Never thought about it," Elkins admitted. He paused for a long moment, then ventured, "But now that you mention it, sure, I got me a theory. See, Mohawk is an Indian name, right?"

"We have established that," Whisters said somewhat impatiently.

"Well, out here in Arizona, this was all Indian territory once, right? But we got us a whole passel of way stations, right? So it seems to me we just plain and simple didn't have enough Indian names of our own to go around. So when they got to namin' this place, they had to import—"

Sally Elkins laughed. "Mr. Whisters, I believe I remember you once said something about hearing a lot of bull on the road, as a salesman?"

Her husband laughed with her. "Dammit, Sally, the man asked for a theory. All theories are bull . . . leastwise, until they get proved, right?"

Whisters nodded enthusiastically. "I accept your theory as well as your view of the scientific method. I also would be pleased to accept some beans, if there's more on the stove. Furthermore, I am pleased to report that our friends from south of the border did not cause any damage to my stock of wares, and therefore"—he reached into his coat and produced a bottle of whiskey—"I would propose that we personally damage this one. Naturally, I shall have to report the damage to my company and complete the necessary expense account forms, but my report will attribute said damage to our attackers. Unless, of course, any of you feel that my doing so would be unethical. Reverend?"

Cull started at the reference to him. He obviously had not been interested in the conversation and instead seemed to be concentrating on consuming as many beans and tortillas as mouth, stomach, and time would allow. "Sir?" he asked, looking confused.

Walt Grader poked his spoon toward the bottle. "He was speakin' of ethics."

"Ethics, sir, are very important," the preacher declared sonorously.

"Fine," Whisters murmured. He pulled the cork of the bottle with his teeth and removed it with a graceful hand. "Glasses for everyone. We drink to ethics." He suddenly looked around. "I say, where is Miss Richmond?"

Sally Elkins placed a tray of glasses on the table. "It's not polite to ask. She's freshening up."

Her husband laughed. "What that means is, she's outside in the—"

"She's freshening up!" Sally repeated.

"She's freshening up," Moses echoed and grinned at his wife.

"To ethics—and to our Mexican friends," Whisters declared, deftly pouring amber liquid into each of the glasses on the tray. "What a boring day this might have been without them!" He glanced at Rado Kane, quipping, "Not to discount the show you put on for us at Yuma, Mr. Kane."

"I didn't aim for that to be a *show*, Mr. Whisters," the gunfighter retorted coolly.

The salesman reacted immediately to Kane's tone of voice. "I didn't mean it the way it sounded," he said apologetically. "No offense meant." He extended a full glass to the gunfighter.

"No offense taken," Kane murmured.

Sam Loomis lifted his glass to his lips and swallowed half its contents. "You peddle good stuff, Whisters. You agree, Reverend?"

The Reverend Cull looked as though he had been about to down the full glass at one swallow. Hearing his name, however, and with all eyes on him, his hand lowered a fraction and he took a small sip of the whiskey. His eyes looking toward heaven—or at least toward the ceiling —he smiled and declared, "The Lord's gift of grains has been well served by whichever distillers produced this liquid . . . although I can't consider myself that much of an expert."

"Maybe not with whiskey, Reverend," Kane remarked, "but you looked fairly expert with a gun this afternoon. Where does a man of the Book get that kind of experience?"

"To every thing, Mr. Kane, there is a season. So says Ecclesiastes." A thin smile appeared on Cull's cadaverous face as he added, "I suggest we all take a moment to thank our Maker for His deliverance of us safely this afternoon." He began to bow his head.

"Hope you don't mind," Walt Grader rejoined, "but

I'll thank Sam and Kane here. I didn't notice our Maker doin' much of the shootin'."

"Don't leave out Mrs. Hallan," Lyman Whisters put in. "She decreased the odds against us by at least one." He smiled at the elderly woman.

"Two," she corrected, smiling back. "If we're allowed to count horses."

Crystal Richmond entered the room, and Sally Elkins indicated the empty chair as she stood and crossed to the stove. "Set yourself down, Miss Richmond. We've got plenty of food left."

"Really, I'm not hungry," Crystal responded, hesitating behind the empty chair between Loomis and Whisters.

"Sit," Moses said, his tone a fatherly sternness. "You need to eat something. By the look of you, you also need to have some of Mr. Whisters's liquid refreshment. It'll warm you up where you need it."

Whisters passed a full glass to her. "He's right. Think of it as medicinal. Good for what ails you."

"What ails us all," Cull remarked as he extended his empty glass to Whisters, who filled it. Turning to the young woman, Cull told her, "I know violence can be upsetting, yet the world is violent and we must accept it. It is a device of Satan, and Satan is a part of God's plan that we must also accept. It may be difficult to understand—"

"I think we all understood perfectly today," Whisters huffed. "A bunch of Mexican bandits wanted to severely curtail our activities. If Satan was one of *them*, I hope one of *us* got him."

Cull stiffened. "One should not make light of the Prince of Darkness," he proclaimed, staring into his whiskey-filled glass. "For he remains ever with us and ever vigilant."

Loomis nodded as if in agreement. "By the same way of thinkin', we shouldn't make light of them Mexicans. They may be remainin' with us, too."

"How do you mean that?" Crystal asked in an unsteady voice.

"Miss, if them *bandidos* have convinced themselves we're carryin' a payroll, they'll no doubt think about tryin' to hit us here. It's logical, since once we leave, they won't know if we're *still* carryin' it or left it here for another stage to carry."

Whisters disagreed. "No, we beat them off back on the road. Not only are there fewer of them now, but there are two more guns here—Moses and Sally. Plus the fact that we've got better cover and a supply of ammunition that could carry us for a medium-sized war. No, attacking us here wouldn't be at all logical."

The shotgunner's eyebrows raised. "Who says Mexicans are logical?"

"Why, you did. You said—"

"I said they'd think about it. Which means *we* should think about it, that's all. Which also means we take turns stayin' awake as a lookout. The last man to turn in, wake me up. I'll determine who's got the next watch and when." Looking from person to person, he suggested, "I'd say get all the rest you can. I'm beginnin' to get a bad feelin' about this run."

He rose from the table and left the main room for the bunk room, where the men would be sleeping. Elkins would join them, with Crystal and Mrs. Hallan taking his place in his and Sally's bedroom.

Whisters poured himself another full glass of whiskey. He turned to Mrs. Hallan and looked at the elderly woman for a long moment, then asked, "And what do *you* think? Will the *bandidos* be attacking us here?"

She gave him a sphinxlike smile. "Why ask me? Mr. Loomis has had far more experience with this sort of thing than I."

Whisters sighed loudly, then looked at the bottle. "Well, perhaps a bit more of this tonic will help me see things more clearly—although probably sleeping would make more sense."

"That's one of the few things we agree upon," Gideon Cull remarked as he rose from the table. "Good night, everyone. I'm getting some much-needed sleep." With his black satchel clutched to his body, he strode from the room, veering at the last moment from the sleeping quarters toward the outhouse.

"I guess I should be retiring, too," Crystal announced to no one in particular, but her eyes made brief contact with Rado Kane's. Sally rose as well, and the two of them left the room.

"Interesting young woman," Whisters observed.

Kane nodded silently, swishing the whiskey that remained in his glass.

"The preacher's interesting, too," Whisters continued as he pulled out his deck of cards and began shuffling them. "Notice how he keeps that bag of his tight under his arm, even when going out to relieve himself? Sets a lot of store by them Bibles, I guess. Interesting. Also interesting how good he is with a gun. Got an eye for the women, too, judging from the way he was staring at Miss Richmond. What do you think about him?"

"Haven't much thought about him at all," the gunfighter admitted.

Whisters looked at Isabel Hallan, then asked, "But you've thought about him, haven't you? I could see you peering at him in the stage, and you were using your piano wire."

She hesitated before speaking. "Yes. I have given the Reverend Mr. Cull some thought. I've given each of you some thought. But I really don't intend to discuss any of my thoughts—if you don't mind, Mr. Whisters." She drank the small amount of whiskey left in her glass and placed it on the table. "It doesn't take much thought, however, to see that my glass is empty. Does that suggest anything to you, Mr. Whisters?"

"Are you seeking my professional services, Mrs. Hallan?" he quipped.

"Indeed I am, Mr. Whisters." She maintained her serious expression for as long as she could—about two seconds—and then her laugh was echoed by the others.

"All right," the salesman said, pouring half the contents of his almost-full glass into Mrs. Hallan's while addressing everyone at the table, "I'll tell you what. It's too early for me to turn in, so how about a little game to while away the time?"

Moses Elkins shook his head. "No little game with you, my friend. Last time you came through, I got to wondering if I was gonna keep my socks."

Whisters then eyed Rado Kane and Walt Grader, but the gunfighter and the driver shook their heads.

Mrs. Hallan rose and looked at Whisters. "I, too, need to get some sleep. But first I would like to compliment you on your display of card tricks this morning. You were quite expert."

"You know your way around a deck?" Whisters asked.

She smiled her knowing smile again. "I will let you be the judge of that. I will turn my back while you deal out sixteen cards facedown in four rows of four, placing the four aces anywhere you wish. When you tell me to turn around again, I will point them out to you." So saying, she turned her back on the table.

Whisters rubbed his jaw. Then, his eyes twinkling, he showed the four aces in his hand to Rado Kane. Kane, in turn, pointed at the card in the top left-hand corner. Whisters replaced it with the ace of hearts, then pointed at Walt Grader. When the ace of spades was placed where the driver had pointed, Moses Elkins designated the position for the ace of clubs. Whisters then displayed the ace of diamonds, and Elkins started to laugh when he saw where it went, but Grader elbowed him to silence.

When the aces had all been placed, the whiskey peddler instructed, "You may turn around now, Mrs. Hallan."

She turned and stared intently at the cards. Then she reached into her bag and brought out her strand of wire and, looping it, twirled it slowly, looking at each of the men around the table and back at the cards. The twirling stopped suddenly, and she used one end of the wire as a pointer.

"There. And there," she said.

Whisters stared openmouthed at her. Kane turned over his ace of hearts and Grader's ace of spades.

"And there." Kane again did the honors, and Elkins's ace of clubs was exhibited.

"One more to go," the woman mused, her eyes staring at the red-backed cards, with the end of the piano wire pausing above each of them in turn. "Ah, yes!" she exclaimed. "There!"

The whiskey salesman's eyes looked as though they might pop out of his head. The end of the piano wire rested on top of the pile of undealt cards, exactly where he had placed the fourth ace.

Mrs. Hallan put away her wire and smiled. "Not much more than a parlor trick, really," she announced. "*Really*," she repeated.

Elkins whistled through his teeth. "That may be so, ma'am, but you could make a fortune with that parlor trick."

She laughed. "No need, Mr. Elkins. I've made my fortune—or at least all I'll ever need."

"How?" Kane asked, his tone serious.

Her tone matching his, she replied, "I help miners find what they're looking for, Mr. Kane. With my help my late husband died wealthy. I couldn't prevent his death, but he lived happily—and so have others. If I help them, I get paid. However, the payment isn't all that important to me anymore."

"You tell them where the ore is?" Grader asked.

"Sometimes. Sometimes, just as importantly, I tell them where it isn't." She shrugged. "Sometimes I'm right."

"You're goin' to Tucson," Grader said. "You gonna do your work there?"

She smiled her mysterious smile. "I have a ticket to

Tucson, Mr. Grader. I may get there or I may not. If I do, I may work there or I may not. If I do, the work I do there may have something or nothing to do with finding metal in the earth. Does that answer your question?"

"Nope," Grader responded, chuckling.

She regarded him briefly, then said to everyone without preamble, "Good night, gentlemen."

As she turned to leave, Rado Kane thought that he had never met such an elusive woman in all his life—with the exception of Crystal Richmond.

Moses Elkins sighed. "Sure could have used that woman once. But if I had, I'd probably still be scraping my fingernails off on some rocks somewhere instead of being here—and I'd probably be without Sally as well."

"You were a gold hunter?" Kane asked in surprise.

Chuckling, Elkins answered, "One of the best . . . or worst, depending how you mean it."

"But you gave it up. Why?"

Nodding toward the women's bedroom, Elkins replied, "Sally, for one thing. And the other is I finally wised up. You may not find my way of life to your liking, Mr. Kane, but I can tell you, I've had my share of traveling, and now I'm happy just being in one place. I like my life and I like my work." He lifted what was left in his glass, then drank it, adding, "And that, gentlemen, was a toast to Mrs. Sally Elkins, a good woman. Without her, I wouldn't like my work or my life much at all. Or my future, for that matter. I'm a good enough fortune teller to know that about myself." Standing, he smiled and said, "No sir, there's nothing like the love of a good woman."

Lyman Whisters watched Elkins as he left the room, then he declared, "As the preacher would say, amen to that."

"Come outside with me for a moment, Miss Richmond," Sally Elkins suggested. "I'd like to have a private chat with you, if you don't mind."

Curious, Crystal followed the older woman out the

back door, and they stood leaning against the building, looking up at the stars for a long moment. Finally the young woman asked, "What is it you wished to tell me? And please, call me Crystal."

"Okay. And you're to call me Sally." She sighed, then said, "I got this real strong sense about you, that you're kind of lost; that you don't know what it is you need."

Smiling in acknowledgment, Crystal commented, "But not you. You know exactly what it is you need, don't you?"

"I sure do. I know what I need, and I've got it—all of it. I've got a good man and a home I truly enjoy. This desert may seem lonely to you, but it's not. There's a whole world out there, and I can see it all, from one horizon to the other. There's a whole lot of life out there, if you look for it—and then there's you, of course."

"Me?"

The older woman chuckled. "Well, you and the other passengers who pass through here like an endless parade. Some get to be good friends—like Sam and Walt, and the other stage people . . . and regulars like Mr. Whisters. Others we get to see just once. But all told, you're a varied lot. Consider Mrs. Hallan, if you will."

Crystal laughed. "I'd certainly agree that she's a varied lot!"

"But a nice woman—at least she seems so. Almost everybody we see is, although there are exceptions." Her tone hardened. "Frankly, I don't find myself having good thoughts about the Reverend Mr. Cull, for example."

"I can't say I care for the man myself," Crystal admitted.

"And then there's Mr. Kane," Sally said quietly.

"You . . . you don't like him?"

"It's not that! Goodness, it's not that at all. Actually, he reminds me of someone, that's all." She fell silent.

Breaking the silence, Crystal finally asked softly, "Was it someone you . . . well, someone you loved?"

"Lord, yes!" Sally declared and burst out laughing. "And still do. Moses! Or, actually, Moses before he finally settled down and got over his gold fever. For almost a full twenty years he chased that yellow metal—and after that, silver—and all that time he had the same restless look about him that your Mr. Kane has."

"*My* Mr. Kane?"

Sally shook her head. "Just a figure of speech, is all." Then she peered at Crystal intently. "Unless there's more to it than that."

The young woman's face flushed. "How could there be? I just met him this morning."

Sally chuckled again. "You're right, of course. But on the other hand, I fell in love with Moses Elkins the first time I ever laid eyes on him. He walked into my father's dry goods store, and bang! It was like being on the wrong end of Sam's shotgun when it goes off." A dreamy expression came over her face. "That was fifteen years ago—and I love him just as much now as I did then."

"That's a wonderful story," Crystal remarked. "And you've been together since then."

"Yes. Through years of gold following, through good times and disappointments, through it all, yes. And for the last four years, right here in this best of all places. Best for me and best for Moses. There's no trace of that old restlessness in him now. The stage line keeps offering him another, bigger station in a real town someplace, but he always says no."

Again Crystal felt the older woman's intense gaze. "You have that look about you, too. That restless look. What gold are you chasing?"

"Is that what I'm doing?"

Sally shrugged. "Maybe not the metal, but I'm sure it's something that probably means to you what gold or silver means to others."

Sighing, Crystal conceded, "Maybe you're right."

"And about Mr. Kane, too? I saw the way you looked at him—and, I'll be bold enough to add, the way he looked at you."

Crystal abruptly stiffened. "That's preposterous! Rado Kane is a professional gunfighter!"

"He is now," Sally agreed, "but he's seeking, same as you."

"But we've hardly exchanged a dozen words!" Crystal protested. She smiled in spite of herself, adding, "A dozen polite words, that is."

Sally smiled with her. "Give it a dozen more, then. Give it a full two dozen, if necessary. What do you have to lose—except maybe everything?"

Chapter Six

The night was clear and moonlit, and despite the few miles that separated him from the station building, Judd Neep could just make out the stagecoach in front of it. It still would be hours before the sun rose, so he had plenty of time to plan how to confront the preacher. At the moment he was more concerned with another problem—or perhaps it presented an opportunity; he did not yet know which it was.

A campfire flickered some three or four miles to the south of the road, more or less opposite the way station. Neep had been watching the campfire grow ever larger as he got nearer. When he had first seen it, he had been pushing the preacher's piebald at a gallop, his mare racing to keep up behind him. But as soon as he had spotted the campfire, he had slowed his mount to a walk. He had not expected to see any signs of humanity out here—other than the way station—and he needed time to think.

His first thought was to ignore the campfire altogether, but then he decided that would not be smart, in case it meant soldiers or lawmen were in the area. If so, it would be important for him to know, for it might affect what plan he came up with to deal with Gideon Cull. The fire could also mean a band of renegade Indians—and that might be trouble in another sense. On the other hand, it could be just a lone drifter warming himself by a fire.

Pulling his newly acquired rifle out of its scabbard

and holding it at the ready, Neep walked his horses slowly along the road. Periodically he stopped and listened, and the third time he stopped, he heard what sounded like several horses. The sounds were not of horses moving but were rather the sounds horses make through their noses and mouths when they are restless. What the young killer could not determine was exactly where the sounds were coming from—whether from the fire or the way-station corral—for sound in the desert could travel long distances.

Turning the piebald off the road, Judd cut a path directly south toward the campfire. He continued in that direction, stopping every five minutes to listen. The horse sounds could be heard just as clearly, but he still could not conclude which direction they were coming from.

Suddenly he thought about his own horses. If he could hear theirs—whoever they might be—they possibly could hear his. His mouth set in a grim scowl, he continued toward the flickering light for a few more minutes, then dismounted quietly and tethered his two animals to a squat creosote bush. With his rifle in hand, he set out on foot, walking as silently as possible.

Finally reaching his destination, he stood some two hundred feet back from the camp and assessed the scene before him: a group of men asleep around the campfire. The sombreros pulled down over the eyes of several of them told him they were Mexicans, but what they were doing there, that far north of the border, Judd had no way of knowing and did not care. "Sometimes," he recalled the preacher saying, "you have to leave well enough alone." This looked to be one of those times.

Retracing his steps back to his horses as quietly as he had come, he led the animals farther away before mounting the piebald and heading back toward the stagecoach way station.

A short while later, his horses again tethered behind him, Judd lay flat on a hillock, intently watching the stage station. He figured he still had four or more hours till daylight, but he could be patient now. After all that distance, after all that time, his quarry was finally at hand, for he was sure that the Reverend Gideon Cull was inside, fast asleep.

Judd's brow suddenly furrowed. It dawned on him that he did not have any further plan. When he and the preacher had been partners, Gideon Cull always did the planning and the thinking. All Judd had to do was follow. *Well*, he thought to himself, *I've followed, all right. Followed him here. But now what?*

Mulling things over, Judd realized that inside the station, along with Cull, were other people, and just how many he could not begin to guess. He had been planning what he would do to the preacher when the two of them were alone—but now he wondered how he would be able to arrange that.

His thoughts were broken off by the sound of loose gravel scraping behind him. Rolling over quickly, he looked up to find that a tall and mustachioed man wearing a sombrero was standing fifteen feet away from him. Each of his hands held a pistol pointed directly at Judd.

"*Buenas noches, señor!*" the man declared with a wide and friendly grin. "I am Juan Carlos Santiago Morales."

Judd Neep stood shirtless in front of the campfire, facing the gang of Mexican bandits. His wrists were bound with rawhide, and the tight knots were biting into his thin flesh.

"I wish you now to speak," the Mexican who called himself Morales announced. "I am pleased that you took my warning seriously back at the way station and have not spoken until I told you that you could. Now it is that time. I will ask questions, and you will answer them."

"Please, I don't want no trouble!" the young man cried.

Ignoring the youth's entreaty, Morales signaled to a tall, fat Mexican. "Lobo," the gang leader said, "take off your sombrero." Obeying, the Mexican took off his hat and laid it carefully on the ground. The hatband was made of a string of black rosary beads that glittered in the firelight.

Judd recognized the beads, for the preacher had once told him about them. He was wondering about their significance when without warning the fat Mexican's fist smashed into the side of his head, and the young killer went down hard, his shirtless torso falling into a cactus. He moaned in pain as the spines stung him like a swarm of bees.

"The desert has many of these cactus plants," Morales remarked calmly as two of his men yanked Judd to his feet, "so we do not have to worry about you using them all up tonight. Besides, I think your back would get used up far before that happens, yes?" Not waiting for an answer, he laughed gleefully, obviously pleased with himself. "Now, my amigo, Lobo will be standing right here by my side to make certain you do not disobey me again. I told you that I would ask the questions and that you would answer them. Although I had not asked a question, you spoke. Do you understand?"

Judd silently glared at him. Morales shrugged, and Lobo's fist again lashed out. Again the youth was thrown into the cactus, and he again moaned as the spines bit into his flesh.

"That was a question," Morales explained once Judd was again standing before him. "But I will assume that you do understand the situation by now. What is your name?"

"J-Judd Neep."

"Very good, señor. And why do you creep around in the night, first to our camp here, and then to the stage-coach station?"

"I—I saw your fire."

"That is no doubt a—how you say?—tribute to your good eyesight. But having seen the fire, why did you come in silence like a thief and then simply go?"

"I—I was hungry, and I thought I could get me some food. But there were too many of you, and I was scared."

Morales nodded thoughtfully. "An intelligent answer. And what of the stage station?"

"Same thing. I was hungry and—"

"Lobo!"

This time Lobo's fist drove into Judd's stomach, doubling him over. The youth dropped to his knees, gasping for breath.

"You see how it is, Señor Neep. I wish only truthful answers. You would not sneak around a stagecoach station if you simply were hungry. You would knock upon their door and ask for some food. Is it perhaps that you wish to steal the payroll money that rightfully belongs to me and my men?"

"No! No!" Judd protested anxiously as he struggled to his feet.

"Then you must tell me what it is that you wish to steal."

"Nothin'! I swear to you!" Judd cried, his face and body soaked with sweat. "Please, I don't want to steal nothin'!"

Morales shook his head and tugged at his mustache. "Lobo begins to get impatient, señor. So I will simply ask you what you want with the stagecoach station."

Swallowing hard, the youth muttered, "I'm followin' somebody."

"Who and why?"

"I—I can't tell you."

"You can't tell me," Morales repeated. "That is your answer?"

"Yes," Judd whispered hoarsely, trying to use his forearm to brush back the tangled thatch of hair that had fallen into his eyes.

Morales nodded, and Lobo's boot kicked Judd's legs out from under him. His back slammed painfully against the gravelly earth, and he groaned.

"I do not like to be kept in the dark, Señor Neep. I also do not like it when my questions are not answered. I would like to remind you that you did not answer my question." He suddenly sighed, adding, "But it is late, and my patience wears thinner even than Lobo's. I believe you will want to tell me all I want to know very soon, señor."

Morales turned and said something quickly in Spanish. Several of the men laughed as one of them rose and walked toward the horses. Suddenly Lobo's hands were at Judd's waist. The youth fought against his captor but could not stop the Mexican from undoing his pants and pulling them down below his knees.

"What are you going to do?" he screeched.

"I do not know if you are familiar with the many wonders of the desert, señor," Morales remarked. "You have had a sample of the cactus plant and know that it can be painful. But the desert has a number of animals, too. Most of them do not like being disturbed, and some of them get very angry when they are. I believe that one of my men has gotten one of these animals very angry."

The man who had left the fire had returned, and in his arms he carried a large piece of rolled-up canvas that clearly contained something struggling to get free. Suddenly the head of the thing poked out of its constraint, and Judd found himself staring at the orange and brown head of a large lizard, its mouth full of small, sharp fangs. The man holding the wriggling canvas abruptly lowered it to a point about a foot above the young prisoner's crotch, and Judd writhed in terror.

Morales grinned, and his white teeth gleamed in the firelight. "This angry creature is very deadly, Señor Neep. However, it takes him a long time to kill. You see, he must chew and chew and chew to get that poison where he wants it. Or, señor, should I say where *I* want it—if I do not begin hearing immediately all that I want to know."

The moon cast a bright light over the landscape outside the way station, and Rado Kane figured it was somewhere near three in the morning. He could easily see the details of the barn, the outhouse, the stage at the front of the building, and the horses in the corral.

Leaning against the corral fence and watching the animals penned inside, he thought how content they looked, even the ones that had pulled the stagecoach through the wild run earlier in the day. Horses had it easy, he decided, even the hard-working ones, for they did not have to think. Over the years Kane had trained himself to be like that, for not thinking was a good habit to have when you did Kane's kind of work.

He recalled Crystal Richmond asking whether his was an honorable profession, and he had given her the answer he had given others—and given himself. But he was not sure he believed it anymore. There was a time when the answer worked just fine, but now more and more frequently it did not work at all. Some of those times were when he thought about Calvin Dunny, and lately he had been thinking about Calvin Dunny more than he wanted to.

Kane had known Dunny only briefly; in fact, he had talked to the man just once, three years ago in a saloon in Leadville.

When Kane had entered the saloon that midmorning, it had been empty except for the bartender and the lone customer who sat at a table with a mug of coffee. The man, in his mid-forties, was tall and lean. His dark suit was clean, his hard face clean-shaven, and the pair of pistols thonged to his thighs were silver plated. Kane recalled feeling the man's eyes sizing him up. Then the man had smiled and asked Kane to join him, and the young gunfighter had accepted the offer, ordering coffee and sitting down at the table.

"You know who I am, son?"

"No. I just rode in," Kane had replied.

"My name is Calvin Dunny."

Kane had heard the name, but he had expected Calvin Dunny to look different. Just how different Kane could not have said, for gunfighters came in all sizes and shapes, even famous ones.

"I've killed twenty men, maybe more," Dunny had remarked casually, then sipped his brew.

"Why are you telling me?" Rado had responded.

Dunny had taken another sip of his coffee, then looked hard at Kane. "Because you just rode into town. Because of the way you carry that gun and the way you carry yourself. If you're here on business—and that business is me—I just thought you ought to be aware."

Kane had nodded: "If I were here on business and that business was you, I'd be aware already."

Laughing, Dunny had rejoined, "I guess that would be so, wouldn't it? What's your name, son—and your head count?"

Kane had told him his name, then had stared intently at the older gunfighter, adding, "I don't keep score."

Again Dunny had laughed. "Not now you don't, maybe. In my early days, I didn't either. But someday you will, and someday you'll start thinking about things. The thinking starts coming on hard just about the time the hands and eyes start to slow up a little. That's when you start thinking about your last gunfight."

Kane's pale eyes had narrowed. Tilting his head slightly, he had asked, "The last one?"

"That's right. Someday one gunfight is gonna be the last, whether you walk away from it or not. That's fact. But that's not what I'm talking about. After a while, you reach a point when every gunfight is gonna be the last one. You'll hang up the guns after this one, you tell yourself. You'll unbuckle that gun belt for good, before somebody else has to do it for you. You'll start using a new name, go to a place where your face won't be recognized, maybe grow a beard like I'm planning on doing."

Pausing, Dunny had signaled the bartender for more coffee. When his and Kane's mugs had been refilled with the steaming brown liquid, the older man had remarked, "That's what I'm talking about."

Kane had asked, "So you've quit?"

Sighing, Dunny had shaken his head. "Not yet, but

almost. After today. Today at noon, I meet a man out in the street. His name's Lucas Root—and Lucas Root is the last. I've made up my mind." The older gunfighter had leaned back and assessed Kane, as if gauging his character. "You know why I'm telling you this?"

"No."

"Two reasons. One, so you can tell others that Calvin Dunny has fought his last, so maybe other men who might be looking to build up their reputations won't give me a thought and will leave me in peace. The second reason is that maybe having told somebody about my decision, I'll stick by it this time." Chuckling, he had declared, "This way of life ain't easy to quit, son. I never had any other, and trying out something completely new is unsettling. This time, though, I mean it." He had smiled sadly and raised his coffee mug in salute. "Wish me luck, Kane."

"I wish you luck," the young gunfighter had responded. "With both things."

"Both?"

Kane had taken a long drink from his coffee mug before replying, "With your plan *and* with Lucas Root."

That day at noon, three shots had been fired out on the street. One of them caught Calvin Dunny in the throat. He had indeed fought his last gunfight.

Now, leaning against the corral fence and staring up at the stars, Rado Kane knew it was his turn to think. He looked again at the horses, deciding they knew a kind of peace no man ever would. They never questioned anything and were content with what they had. He watched them, with their economy of movement and sound, and thought how different that was from man as well.

Suddenly something behind him both moved and made a sound. Kane whirled, his cocked Colt out of his holster and pointing directly at the cause of the movements. "Damn," he breathed, easing the hammer back in place and pushing the weapon back into leather. "Never, *never* sneak up behind an armed man like that, Miss Richmond."

Crystal stood frozen a dozen feet from him, her eyes huge with fright. "I didn't mean—"

"It doesn't matter what you meant. It still could have gotten you killed. Especially since I'm expecting Mexicans to be sneaking up behind me."

She took a few steps closer. "I'll remember that. I will. It's just—"

He sighed again. "I'm sorry I barked at you. Are you all right, Miss Richmond?"

She smiled thinly. "I shouldn't say so, no. I don't feel right at all. I couldn't sleep, and when I saw you out here I thought . . . well, I thought—"

"You thought what?"

Looking down at her feet, she murmured, "I wanted to say some things to you, that's all. But I haven't gotten off to a very good start, have I?"

He chuckled. "No. But not all that bad, either. At least you're talking to me."

Pulling her shawl tighter around her shoulders, the young woman stepped closer. When they were within touching distance she moved to his left and leaned against the corral, facing the horses. "They look so beautiful, don't they? I mean, here, under the stars and in the moonlight. Today they were just—well, just animals. But now there's something almost magical about them. And that's true of the land and the sky, too."

Kane nodded. "You do get a lot of good sky for your money out here."

Crystal laughed softly. "That's the first thing I really noticed about your 'out here' that moved me in a positive way. Chicago skies aren't like this at all. There's always something between you and the sky. Buildings or smoke or both." She broke off abruptly and faced her companion. "Mr. Kane, I'd like to apologize to you."

"There's no need," he said quietly.

"Oh, but there is!" she declared, nodding. "I shouldn't have rushed into judging you the way I did. I guess I now fully appreciate the fact that, if you chose, you could have easily killed that boy back in Yuma. It wasn't until we were attacked and I saw how well you could shoot anything you really aimed at that—"

"Apology accepted," he cut in.

She smiled warmly at him. "Thank you. I also hope you'll accept my thanks for saving us today."

Kane smiled self-consciously, then suddenly remembered he was wearing his hat. With a less than deft movement, he took it off, exposing his thick dark hair. "Don't give me so much credit, Miss Richmond. After all, I had a lot of help today."

"Please, it's Crystal. Yes, I know you did. I don't mean to make you uncomfortable. I just wanted to tell you that, in spite of the way I acted before, I really am glad that you're on this trip."

Kane's eyes went from hers to his hat. Grinning, he held it up so she could see the small round hole in the brim, then joked, "My hat has reason to question your statement."

Clearly mortified, Crystal replied, "Oh, I can't tell you how terrible I feel about that! I could have shot you instead of your hat, you know."

"The thought had occurred to me," Kane agreed dryly. "Maybe you ought to have a lesson or two on using a gun."

"No, please. I appreciate the offer, but guns represent a real evil to me."

Shrugging, he responded, "Guns aren't evil or good. It's the people on either end of them that are. But the offer stands."

Crystal said nothing, and silence fell between them. Her eyes drifted again to the sky, then to the desert around them. "It looks so different at night," she remarked again. "Today I was thinking how ugly it all looked, how dry and dead and desolate. But now, like this, it's more alive. Quiet and peaceful, to be sure, but alive."

"There's a lot of life on the desert," Rado acknowledged.

"That's exactly what Sally Elkins said to me about

living out here by herself." Crystal laughed. "Of course, she also pointed out that with Moses she was far from being here by herself. She said the work isn't always easy, but it's interesting—that is, the people are interesting. They get to meet a whole lot of different people without having to go anywhere. She also said the stage company is always looking for men to manage their stations. It doesn't take a lot of training and—"

"Excuse me, Miss Richmond," Kane interrupted, "are you trying to change my line of work?"

The blood rushed to Crystal's face, and she was obviously embarrassed. "Oh! Oh, no! I was just mentioning—"

"Yeah. Well, you forgot something kind of important," the gunfighter remarked with a look of irony on his face. "It just so happens that Moses was telling Whisters and me about his work, and he agreed he had a good job and a good life. But the key is having a good woman to share both." The look of irony grew into a grin as he added, "Now, I don't happen to have a woman at all, not to mention a good one. I might consider all you've been saying if you could arrange that part of it for me. You know any good woman who might want to settle down and share a life with an ex-gunfighter?"

She looked at him steadily for a long moment, then asked softly, "Do you want to be an ex-gunfighter?"

"I've given it some thought," he admitted, then fell silent.

Crystal took a step closer and murmured, "I don't know a lot about you, obviously, but I'd like to. I'd like to understand—"

"How Rado Kane became a man of the gun?" he finished for her.

"Yes. Among other things. For example, your name, Rado. Colorado was what that boy called you. Is it your real name?"

He looked into the distance, his eyes not focused on anything. "My folks came west from St. Louis with nothing much more than their willingness to work hard and settled in Colorado, working their own small farm. I was the youngest of three brothers, and each of us was named after the town or the territory we were born in. Tip, Kearney, and Colorado. My pa used to say that his boys were living evidence of this country's greatness. He was proud, real proud, of Ma and his sons."

"Was?" Crystal asked softly.

Kane's eyes stayed where they had been, but his face stiffened slightly. "The war took all three of us from the farm—and I was the only one who came back. Tip died from a Confederate cannonball in Virginia somewhere and Kearney from gangrene in Tennessee, or so they said. When I got back, Ma and Pa were dead from cholera, and the farm belonged to somebody else, all legal and proper. I wouldn't have stayed even if I could have claimed the land."

"The hurt was that deep?" she asked, her voice tender.

Kane shifted his position uncomfortably. His eyes snapped to hers and he admitted, "I'm not used to talking about myself much. Why don't you talk about you?"

She gave him a small smile. "It's too bad you were asleep when I told my life story to Mr. Whisters."

"I wasn't," he retorted, smiling crookedly.

Looking slightly startled, Crystal said, "Then you know what there is to know."

He nodded, amending, "Except why you finally decided to leave San Francisco."

She closed her eyes for a moment. "California was a lot more than I had bargained for, and I wasn't used to the brutality. In the end it came down to buying and selling—dollars for flesh. The man who owned the dance hall where I was working decided he wanted to own me, too. I—I couldn't do that. When he put the proposition to me very bluntly, I had to leave."

"For Tucson."

"As you probably heard me tell Mr. Whisters, I have a friend there, an older woman. Annie Gantlin is her name. I met her when she, too, worked in San Francisco, and she always talked about how she'd like to start a real theater, a legitimate theater. She moved to Tucson and apparently has come into a bit of money—although I don't know how—because she wrote asking if I wanted to join her in her venture. I wrote back telling her yes, two days before I left San Francisco." Crystal suddenly giggled. "I suppose it's possible that my letter may not get there much before I do. I certainly hope I'm not that much of a surprise for her."

Rado Kane studied her face carefully, then remarked in a wry voice, "I hope, Miss Richmond—"

"Crystal, please."

"—Crystal. I hope that your plans work out in Tucson." Then he told her, "I think we'd both best turn in now. Tomorrow's going to be another very long, very hot day."

She nodded, then turned and walked slowly toward the adobe building. He stood where he was, watching her, and after three steps, she looked back over her shoulder and smiled at him. "Good night . . . Rado."

"Good night to you, Crystal."

Chapter Seven

Rado Kane was instantly awake at the sound of the gunshot. He rolled out of his bedroll and onto the bare floor of the main room of the station, where he had finished off what was left of the night after having roused Lyman Whisters for the watch after his own. He had decided not to fight the chorus of snores in the bunk room, and he had also decided to stay in his clothes, except for his boots, which stood supporting his holstered Colt inches to the right of his head.

Less than three seconds separated the second shot from the first, but by the time it sounded, Kane's gun was in his hand and he was crawling to the small window at the side of the building's main entrance. The bunk room door banged open behind him, and two figures in underwear spilled into the main room, both carrying rifles.

"Is it them Mexicans, Kane?" Walt Grader asked. The driver hunkered down beside the gunfighter and peered out the small window.

"I can't see anyone yet," Kane replied as the third shot fired.

"Damn! The horses!" Sam Loomis declared urgently. "I'll go check out the corral! Send Moses out after me!"

"I'm here," Moses Elkins said as he hurried into the main room, pulling on his pants. He followed Loomis outside, passing Lyman Whisters rushing in as he did.

The liquor peddler hurried to Kane's side, looking

slightly embarrassed as he hastily tucked his shirt into his checkered trousers. "I didn't see anything, so I figured it was okay to go use the outhouse, even though I was on watch." He then echoed Grader's query, asking, "Is it the Mexicans?"

"Can't tell until they show themselves," Kane answered. "But the guns don't sound all that close."

"Close enough for me," Grader commented, taking a new position at the side window that enabled him to see the barn and part of the corral. "Hmph," he sniffed. "Only thing I see out there is Sam."

He had barely finished speaking when two more shots rang out, followed by three more in close succession. Then the air was filled with a barrage of cracking gunfire that lasted about twenty seconds, during which time Kane counted five ricochets off the front and sides of the adobe station. Finally it fell quiet.

"Thunder and damnation!" the Reverend Gideon Cull shouted as he came into the room, breaking the silence. He was fully dressed in his all-black clothes, including boots and hat and the ever-present satchel pinned under his left arm. His revolver was in hand. "What in the name of the Lord—"

"While you're up, Preacher," Kane cut in, "get some shells for Grader." Then, looking at Whisters, he indicated the peddler's pistol. "Do you have more ammunition for that?"

"Only a few in a box in the bunk room."

"Cull, get Mrs. Elkins to show you where they keep the cartridge boxes," Kane ordered sharply. "Then get us all supplied, including yourself." Nodding toward his bedroll, he added, "And while you're at it, toss me my boots and gun belt."

"And just who put you in charge, gunfighter?" Cull demanded. He had not moved from his initial position near the bunk room door.

"I did, just now," Walt Grader answered. "As driver, I'm entitled. So haul your butt, Reverend."

Cull crossed to where Kane's boots and gun belt lay on the floor and sent them to the gunfighter's right with a kick from his own boot. The plainsman's hat then followed.

"What are they waitin' for?" Grader asked nervously, straining his neck to see as much as he could from the window. "Damned odd attack, I'd say."

"I'd have to agree," Whisters mused. Turning to Kane, he remarked, "I'd have thought they'd try to get as close to us as they could—maybe even try to get inside the place—while we slept."

Kane pulled on his left boot, then his right. Reaching to where his hat lay on the floor, he had it halfway to his head when a gunshot roared and it flew out of his hand. Whipping around, gun aimed, Kane found himself staring at Crystal Richmond, who stood staring at him. She was fully but hastily dressed, framed in the doorway of the Elkinses' bedroom, with Billy Nathan's smoking gun in her hand. Her eyes were wide, and her face was a mixture of fear and embarrassment.

"It just went off," she choked hoarsely. "By itself, sort of."

Kane looked at the new hole in his hat, this one in the rear of the crown. Then his eyes narrowed, and he growled, "Lady, I don't care what you say. When this is over, like it or not, you're getting some shooting lessons— before you kill off all the good guys."

"Kane!" Whisters suddenly shouted, gesturing with his pistol barrel toward the window.

The gunfighter looked outside and his body tensed. "Now we know the reason for all the gunfire," he observed. "It was to wake us up."

"Got to admit, it worked," Grader muttered, scowling.

Everyone scurried closer to the front window and cautiously peered outside to see two riders leading their horses at a walk toward the adobe station. One of them, large both in height and girth, was periodically waving a white cloth high above the sombrero on his head. As they came closer it was clear that he was leading the other

horse by its reins, and the second rider—hatless and thin
to the point of being gaunt—seemed as though he could
barely stay in the saddle.

Rado Kane watched their approach silently for a few
moments, then asked Walt Grader, "See anything on your
side?"

"Nothin'," the driver replied, shaking his head.
"Whisters, go out back and holler to Sam and Moses and
see if they've spotted somethin'. And where in hell's that
ammo?"

"I've got it," Sally Elkins responded from her bedroom doorway. "I wanted to make sure Mrs. Hallan was
all right and that Miss Richmond was safely tucked away
so she wouldn't get hurt . . . or hurt anybody. And, unless
anybody objects, I'm also going to put some coffee on."

"Hmm. Interesting," Kane mumbled.

Lyman Whisters, his hand on the doorknob, turned
and stared at him. "The coffee?"

Giving the peddler a stern look, Kane retorted, "No,
our Mexican friend there. Yesterday, none of the bandits
had rifles. Now this one does—although he's using it as
the flagpole for his white shirt."

"Maybe it's broken," Whisters offered.

Kane shrugged. "Maybe. One sure thing, the other
rider's no Mexican—unless they're building them with
blond hair these days."

A sudden sharp gasp sounded from directly behind
the gunfighter, and he swiveled his head to see Gideon
Cull's eyes bulging, while his left arm tightened even
firmer on his satchel. Extending the pistol gripped in his
right hand out the open window, the preacher exclaimed,
"You get the Mexican, Kane, and I'll get the other one!"

"Put the gun down, Cull," Kane ordered, his voice
cold. "Keep it ready, but put it down. Now!"

"But—"

"No buts. Every step they're taking makes them better targets." Kane's tone was mocking as he added, "Besides, the man's showing a flag of truce. Surely you, a man

of God, wouldn't violently trample such a declaration of peace, would you, Reverend?"

Cull's hand shook as he obeyed, but his eyes were still bulging. Suddenly he seemed to snap out of his shock, and he challenged Kane. "You honor such a thing from men like that?"

"Don't forget, they could have tried to get a lot closer to us while we slept. It's clear they want to talk, so we'll talk. If they want to start shooting after we talk, *then* we'll shoot." Gesturing toward the bunk room, he suggested, "If you want to make yourself useful, Preacher, go keep watch from the back window, just in case these two have some other pals with them."

Cull had just disappeared into the bunk room when Whisters came back in, followed by Sam Loomis and Moses Elkins. "Apparently our two approaching friends are the only ones out there," the peddler said.

Nodding, Loomis confirmed, "Yep, and they didn't do nothin' to any of the horses."

Whisters walked across the room, joining Kane at the window. "Now that's something real interesting," he announced in a bemused voice.

Rado Kane gave his companion a quick glance, then asked, "What is? The Mexican or the other one? He looks kind of young from here."

"Neither man. It's the horse, the one the skinny guy is riding. I think I've seen that piebald before—just yesterday, in fact."

Kane looked more closely at the horse. The riders were less than fifty yards from the front of the station, and he could see them and their mounts clearly. Shaking his head, he said, "It doesn't ring a bell."

"Unless I miss my guess, it should—a church bell," Whisters quipped. "Among other things, I know my horseflesh, and if that nag isn't the one the good Reverend Cull left in the Adonde corral, then it's a mighty close twin."

"Adonde?" a woman's voice asked. Kane turned to see Isabel Hallan enter the room with a pistol in her hand and an odd expression on her face.

"Nothing to concern you, ma'am," Kane said reassuringly. Then he indicated the weapon. "I see you held on to Sam's gun."

She nodded absently. "Yes. I thought I'd keep watch from our bedroom window. But I need some shells."

"On the table," the gunfighter responded, pointing toward the box with his own gun. Mrs. Hallan quickly reloaded, then returned to the women's bedroom, and Kane returned his attention to the window.

"That's Cull's horse, Kane," Whisters persisted. "I'll give you three-to-one odds on it."

Kane did not comment. Whether Whisters was right was of little concern to him. There were more important things that claimed his attention. "Since your eyes are so good, Whisters, focus them on the younger man's hands."

The peddler did as he was told and his eyes widened in surprise. "They're tied together and lashed to the saddle horn. And look at the bruises on the lad's face." When the riders had closed to thirty yards, he remarked, "I'd say that young man doesn't look like he especially wants to be here."

The riders halted some fifteen yards from the building, and the Mexican waved his white flag of peace. "You inside!" he shouted. "I want to talk!"

Kane turned toward Loomis. "Keep that shotgun at the ready."

"You bet," Loomis responded. "'Sides, I got a bone to pick with that Mexican. Nobody attacks my stage and gets off scot-free."

"Hey, gringos!" The bandit's heavily accented voice suddenly split the air. "Do you not hear? Did we not wake you up enough?"

The peddler watched the Mexican for a moment, then remarked to Kane, "Seems like the man's getting a bit edgy."

Kane squared his hat on his head. "Well, let's not get him irritated. Cover me. Sam, Moses, wait a few moments, then follow me outside. I'm gonna go see what our amigo has in mind."

"*Vaya con Dios*," Lyman Whisters said as Rado Kane started toward the door.

The gunfighter paused in his tracks and turned to look at the liquor salesman. "I wish you'd said that in another language," he said dryly. Then he cocked both hammers of the shotgun and stepped through the door.

"It is about time, gringo!" Juan Morales shouted impatiently. "My friend and I, we wish to dismount and come forward to speak with you. What do you say?" He again waved the white flag.

"Dismount," Kane instructed, gesturing slightly with the rifle that was pointed directly at the bandit. "Then walk your horses straight toward me, very slowly. And raise that flag as high as you can. Now!"

The Mexican lifted the rifle in his right hand up a foot, and the flag flapped in the morning breeze. Then the bandit brought his right leg over the pommel and slid gracefully from his horse to the ground. Stepping slowly to the side of the second horse, he untied a knot on his captive's saddle horn, then yanked on the thong binding the young man's wrists. Judd Neep fell to the ground in a crashing heap.

Turning to Kane, Morales smiled broadly and remarked, "My companion, he lacks something in—how you say?—agility."

Ignoring the jibe, the gunfighter growled, "Move real slow," and took three steps forward himself. He heard the door open behind him, and within moments Sam Loomis and Moses Elkins were flanking him, their rifles also pointed at the Mexican.

"Hey, what is with all these weapons?" the Mexican asked, flashing a toothy grin and gesticulating with his hands. "Señors, I am Juan Carlos Santiago Morales. Put away your guns, my friends. I come in peace. I come to—how you say?—negotiate."

"Just keep that right arm high," Kane warned. "Moses, take their horses. Sam, kindly take that, uh, flagpole—and any other weapons they've got."

The men did as they were bid, and as Elkins led the piebald past the shotgunner toward the corral, Loomis took a long look at the horse. Kane noticed the look, then addressed the bandit and his prisoner. "Now, amigos, keep your hands high and step inside."

With a jab of his shoulder, the Mexican shoved the straw-haired youth into the station house. As Judd Neep passed Kane, the gunfighter looked closely at the bruises and cuts on his face. Somebody had beaten him badly.

Once the duo was inside, Kane ordered, "Sit. Both of you. On the floor."

Morales protested to Kane, "What you ask me to do is undignified."

Kane nodded in agreement. "I suppose that's right, Morales. I suggest, though, you do what I say—before I put a bullet between your dignified eyes."

Morales sat, and the gangly youth did likewise. Judd's face showed no emotion until a footfall behind him made him turn his head to look over his shoulder. Kane noticed a narrowing of the boy's eyes as Reverend Gideon Cull stepped into the room, and while the preacher had recovered quickly, Kane had not missed the split-second freeze when Cull's eyes fell on the boy.

Looking back at the bandit, Kane found the man studying him. Finally Morales said, "Now, I will tell you why it is that I have come."

Shaking his head, Kane responded, "Not yet. There are more of us." He turned to Cull and instructed, "Tell the women to come in here." When Crystal Richmond, Isabel Hallan, and Sally Elkins had entered the room, the gunfighter nodded to Morales. "Now you get to say your piece."

The Mexican spread his hands. "It is simple. I have come for the payroll. That is all I wanted to get from you yesterday, and that is what I want from you today."

"As simple as that," Kane echoed, his pale blue eyes boring into the bandit's dark brown ones.

Morales smiled. "It is a simple solution to our problem, yours as well as mine. You must understand that my men out there—and rest assured they are out there, although you cannot see them—they are foolish. They wish to shoot at everyone all the time and make everyone their enemy. I, Juan Carlos Santiago Morales, wish to make no man my enemy . . . at least, not without necessity."

He stopped, and his face took on a look of complete puzzlement as he watched Isabel Hallan begin to manipulate her piano wire. She, in turn, was looking at him and at the younger man through narrowed eyes.

"That," he remarked slowly, "would make a good garrote for strangling someone." He smiled at the elderly woman, but she did not smile back.

"You were saying," Kane prompted, "that you don't like making enemies."

The Mexican sighed deeply. "In truth, señor, I do not. All I wish for is the payroll the stagecoach carries, nothing more than that. Which makes me, perhaps, the enemy of the stagecoach company but not an enemy of yourself or of these other fine passengers."

"Attacking the stagecoach yesterday was a odd way of making friends," Kane observed.

Morales sighed again. "You are right, señor. And there are several dead men and more wounded ones who can testify to the foolishness of that approach. Or at least the wounded ones can testify." Stroking his thick mustache, he glanced at Gideon Cull and added, "Maybe the others, too, if they are in a place where such things are possible. What do you think, Holy Father?"

"They are roasting in the fires of hell!" the preacher replied sternly to the bandit, but his eyes never strayed from the youth.

"Perhaps," the Mexican said with a shrug. "But let us leave the dead to the dead and leave yesterday to yesterday. One cannot undo the things of the past. Today is today, and my proposal is that the payroll be turned over to me right now. Once that has happened, I and my foolish men will be on our way, never to trouble you again."

"Until the next payroll?" Sam Loomis asked, his voice a cold growl. Holding the makeshift flag in his hands, he crossed in front of the two men seated on the floor and handed the rifle to Kane. "Look at the engraving," he instructed the gunfighter in a strained tone.

Examining the rifle, Kane immediately saw why Loomis's voice was strained. The 1866 Winchester .44 was one he had seen before, back at the Adonde station. As he regarded the engraving of the animal that old Bush had speculated was a pregnant elk, Rado Kane told himself that the odds were extremely small that a person would run across two guns like that two days in a row.

The gunfighter stared at the Mexican. "This weapon," Kane said to Morales. "Tell me about it."

The Mexican shrugged again. "That is part of the—how you say?—bonus I bring you as part of our negotiation." Pointing at the blond youth, he then grinned at Kane and said, "He is the other part of the bonus, and the rifle is his. And he admitted that he was following the stagecoach." He then gestured expansively, asking, "Now, what do you say?"

Kane looked at the captive. "What's your name?"

"Judd Neep," came the sullen reply. The young man hardly parted his lips to speak and continued to stare blankly ahead, not acknowledging Kane's presence.

"Is what Morales says right? Is this gun yours?"

Morales replied quickly, "It is! I always speak the truth! This young one, though, he is *mucho* closed of the mouth, but look at those eyes of his. They are like the eyes of a snake. Those are the eyes of someone not to be trusted, believe me. I do not know where he came from or why he was pursuing you, but I have no doubt that he had in mind some harmful intent. Unfortunately, he has been very unwilling to share this secret with me—even after many attempts to persuade him."

Rado Kane abruptly turned and faced Gideon Cull. "Reverend, this young man was riding a piebald horse that's now back in the corral. I want you to take a good look at the animal and tell me if it's the horse you sold at Adonde."

Cull started to move, then stopped. "There's no need for me to look. It was mine," he acknowledged.

"Adonde," Crystal Richmond murmured, looking thoughtful. Then she turned to Isabel. "Mrs. Hallan, when we were there, you said—"

"Yes," the old woman cut in. She ran a hand through her white hair and sighed. "I said it to you—but I should have said something to Mr. Bush as well."

Kane studied the two women carefully for a long moment. He was about to ask them what they were referring to when Lyman Whisters stepped forward and commented to Morales, "There were no rifles when you and your men attacked us yesterday."

Morales clapped his hands. "Aha, you are right, señor! If I had had a rifle—just one rifle like this one here— things might have turned out *mucho* different." He grinned, then pointed at Judd. "But now I have this young one to use as a negotiating tool instead of a rifle." Eyeing Kane, he asked, "What do you say, señor?"

Kane answered, "Sure, we'll take your prisoner off your hands—but we still have you to deal with."

"Correct. But only until you give me the payroll money. What do you say?"

Kane smiled. "How about there is no payroll?"

The Mexican scowled. "That is not negotiating in good faith, señor. Everyone knows the stagecoaches carry payroll money. This is, after all, why Juan Carlos Santiago Morales and his band of foolish friends came up from the south."

"Suppose," Sam Loomis interjected, "that this particular stagecoach carried no payroll?"

Morales shook his head. "That would be a very unfortunate suppose—and one I could not ask my men to believe. If I asked them to do so, my credibility would suffer, and what is a leader without credibility?"

"Alive, maybe," Kane answered offhandedly.

The bandit glared at him. "You do not fully understand. If you insist there is no payroll money or if I do not
leave here alive and well, then some of my followers
might decide to wait until the stagecoach leaves and then
burn this place to the ground in order to search for the
money they believed was left behind. And then they
would regroup with more men and attack the stagecoach
once again . . . and search it with great thoroughness," he
added ominously.

He looked at Crystal and smiled. "No doubt they
would have to kill everybody—even innocent passengers
like the beautiful señorita—and take what valuable things
they have as well. This is not what I would call a satisfactory solution."

"I'd agree with that," Kane said harshly.

The bandit threw open his hands. "So, if you continue to insist to me there is no payroll money, we are at
what is called an unfortunate impasse, no?"

"No," the gunfighter countered, a sly smile spreading
over his face. "There's no impasse because you'll be riding
on the stage with us—as one of the innocent passengers."
He turned to the driver, asking, "Walt, do you have any
problem with that?"

"None whatsoever," Walt Grader replied, grinning.
"And the kid comes, too. He stays with Sam and me until
we find a good jail and somebody finds out exactly what
happened at Adonde."

Lyman Whisters laughed and declared, "You're quite
a good negotiator after all, Morales. Free passage for both
you and your, uh, friend."

The Mexican regarded Whisters coldly, then said to
Kane, "I have considered this idea very carefully, and I do
not think it to be a good one."

"That's too bad, 'cause it's your only choice," Kane
retorted. "Now, how do we get word to your men that
we're taking you—and the payroll—with us?" He winked
at Moses Elkins, saying, "No sense leaving all that nonex-
istent money behind."

Morales muttered, "Fire one shot. That will bring all my men here very fast."

"How about something less hostile?"

"I suppose I could signal from the doorway that just one of my men should approach."

"That sounds better. Do it."

The Mexican frowned and did not move.

Kane gestured toward the doorway, snapping, "Do it now."

Morales regarded the gunfighter. "I have understood your wish. However, the problem is, I do not know what to say to my men. I cannot admit to being captured, for a good leader does not allow himself to be captured."

Kane moved the business end of Loomis's shotgun to within an inch of Morales's forehead. "I can appreciate your difficulty. Perhaps we should go back to that hostile plan of yours . . . and fire that one shot."

Looking much more willing, Morales promised, "I will think of something."

Rado Kane gave the bandit another sly smile. "Now, how did I know you would do precisely that?"

Chapter Eight

The activity at the Gila Bend saloon was unusual for midmorning. More than thirty men and six women—wives of five of the men plus Mary Grogan, who owned and ran the hotel—milled about the room. That any women were even in the place was odd in itself, as was the fact that aside from the town locals half the men in the saloon were Mallory employees. It was downright extraordinary that everybody was drinking for free. But it was, after all, a far from ordinary occasion: Tom Clancy's wake.

Seth Garlath had ruled that the place was open to all, and it was Garlath who was paying the drinking bill. Taking advantage of the mineowner's largesse, the workers sat around—the Mallory men and the Garlath men—in harmonious agreement about their slain co-worker.

"Tom Clancy was a good man and a gentle man," Hawk Brown said from behind the bar as he pushed three glasses of beer to three thirsty miners to his right. " 'It's the good that die young,' my dear old mother used to say, God bless her soul."

"Your dear old mother, was it?" Mrs. Grogan snapped, impatiently tucking a stray strand of her gray-streaked brown hair into her no-nonsense bun. She was in her late forties, and while she was not a tall woman, in build and demeanor she was what polite gentlemen called formidable. Regarding the barkeep with a look of disgust, she then asked Brown, "And did your dear old mother also happen to be mentioning that the good shouldn't be dyin' at all by the gun? Especially in the presence of him who calls himself the town marshal?"

"Don't you be skinning Hawk for what happened," one of the miners—a Mallory man—admonished the hotel owner. "We all know who done it, and we all know there weren't much Hawk could've done to stop it. Except maybe get shot himself, and that wouldn't have stopped nothin', just delayed it."

"And not by much," a Garlath man added. "I was here yesterday and saw the whole thing."

"Did you know Tom Clancy?" Mrs. Grogan asked the man.

"Sure I did. Not well, but I knew him. Like Hawk said, he was a good man."

The woman peered at the man through narrowed eyes. "But you did nothin' to stop the shootin'." She gazed around the saloon, her expression reproachful. "None of the fine and upright and decent men here did anything at all to stop it."

The man she had been talking to remained silent, concentrating on his beer.

"That's a bit unfair, ma'am," Clay Brock said, his tall, muscular body stiffening slightly. The Garlath foreman set his empty beer glass on the bar, then requested, "Give me something a bit stronger, Hawk." Turning again to the woman, he told her, "These men ain't gunfighters, and you know damn well there ain't none of us can face down a man who is."

"Maybe not with a gun," she replied scornfully. "Tom Clancy didn't try it with a gun, either." She turned to the bartender and snapped, "Tell me, Mr. Marshal Brown, wouldn't anyone—even your dear old mother—call that murder?" She sniffed with distaste, then stabbed a finger at Brock. "How many guns does Sandeen carry?"

"One. At least, that's all I ever seen. But that's all he needs."

"And how many bullets might he be havin' in this one gun?"

"Six. You know that."

"I do. And I know where Sandeen is right now. Do you?"

"Sure. He's in the back room with Garlath. Mallory's back there, too, and so are their kids."

Mrs. Grogan smiled. "Well, then. If Sandeen has one gun with six bullets, suppose thirty or twenty or fifteen or even seven real men decided they wanted him either dead or out of town with both arms broken. Who do you think would win?"

Brock shook his head. "I can count as well as you."

"And?"

"And . . . and I repeat, we ain't gunfighters. Maybe not as many as six, but one or two of us would wind up like Tom Clancy. That ain't no way to die."

"Maybe, Mr. Clay Brock, it ain't no way to live, either." She laughed suddenly. "You know what's funny, what surely is a thing that's real funny? Back in the East, the city people there are all the time readin' these stories about how all us people out here are really somethin' to admire. We crossed the great deserts. We beat back the hair-scalpin' Indians. We built up farms and ranches and mines and towns from nothing at all. We're held up as examples of all great things, like dedication to principles, to truth, to self-reliance, to heroism. The real truth is we ain't nothin' of the kind. You, Mr. Clay Brock, and you, *Marshal* Brown, and"—she gestured expansively at the other men in the barroom—"all the rest of you are absolutely nothin' of the kind. Not when one man with one gun with only six bullets can tell all of you what you can and can't do."

"That's a real nice speech, Mrs. Grogan," Let Cutler, Angus Mallory's foreman, remarked, his deeply tanned face darkening angrily, "but I wouldn't speak it too much louder. I don't think Sandeen would think twice about pulling the trigger on you."

"Oh, really?" she asked, her tone dry. "He'd think more than twice, I can be assurin' you of that. Who do you think would be givin' him his meals and his fresh bed linens at the hotel?"

Cutler blinked, then caught the joke. "All right, I'll agree with you there—but you're wrong about another thing. Sandeen may be able to tell some people they can't come into this place and drink, he can do that. But he can't tell us we've got to work."

"I don't understand," Mary Grogan said, puzzled.

Clay Brock drank the shot glass of whiskey Hawk had placed before him in one swallow, then answered for Cutler, "He's talking about work in the mines. There ain't gonna be none. Not until Sandeen quits town. That's not just at the Garlath mine, but Mallory's, too. And that's not just talk, that's plain fact."

Hawk rubbed the bridge of his beaklike nose for a moment, then asked, "You've both agreed to that?"

"Yep, us and our men," Brock replied, nodding. "Tom Clancy shouldn't have died—and nobody else is gonna be second."

"What did Garlath and Mallory have to say about it?" Hawk asked.

"Garlath didn't like it much," Brock answered, chuckling.

"Mallory didn't exactly clap hands either," Cutler added. "But he's all het up on his shooter coming here and solving everything. Rado Kane, his name is. Supposed to be hitting town on today's stage—at least that's what Mallory thinks."

"Which ain't no solution," Brock said. "This Kane comes to town, and maybe he even kills Sandeen, but so what? Then we still got us a gunfighter in Gila Bend, only now the rules say Garlath's crewmen don't get to come into town and drink Hawk's gutwash instead of Mallory's."

"Or," Cutler put in, "it goes the other way, and Sandeen is still in charge. Like Clay says, either way it's bad news. So the only clear solution is to get rid of Sandeen now, and when this Kane shows up, tell him there's no work for him in Gila Bend either."

Hawk nodded, and a smile lit his thin face. "And you told this to your bosses?"

Brock first pointed toward his empty glass. "Another, if you please," he requested. After taking a sip, he finally answered, "Sure, we told our bosses. Thing is, their kids have been telling them the same thing ever since Sandeen first showed up. But stubborn old cusses that they are, they didn't listen."

Downing his beer, Cutler promised, "Now they either listen, or nothing happens in the mines . . . in neither of them."

"I think they mean it," David Garlath stated. He sat with his father and Angus Mallory at the round table in the back room that was usually reserved for very private poker games. Katherine Mallory stood behind her fiancé, her hands on his shoulders. Across the room stood a relaxed Jack Sandeen, slowly sipping a glass of whiskey. "There'll be no work in either of the mines until this gets settled," David concluded.

Angus Mallory's eyes narrowed. "Won't be no work today, anyhow. What with all the drinking goin' on, nobody'll be fit for it."

"And tomorrow?" David asked.

"We'll see about tomorrow when tomorrow comes," Seth Garlath grumbled, his face sullen.

"See about it *now*," Katherine told the mineowner. "You know what the men want. They made it plain enough—plain enough so that even you and my father should be able to understand. Pay Sandeen what you have to, and have him leave town. Now."

Sandeen's lopsided smile twitched. "Who invited her back here?"

"I did," David replied adamantly.

"You," Sandeen growled from the other side of the room, "take a lot on yourself, young pup."

Seth Garlath stood. "Hold it right there, Sandeen. The boy's right. The girl's right, too. Nobody was supposed to get killed—none of the men on either side. You were supposed to make sure Mallory's men didn't start anything, that's all. Threaten them maybe, and maybe at the most wound one or two of them so they'd keep out of our way. But nobody was supposed to get killed."

Sandeen's expression turned hard, and he challenged, "So I leave. Then what? Rado Kane just might not be in the mood to go so quietly, comin' all the distance he has."

"Suppose he didn't come?" Katherine asked.

Nodding, David continued, "Then there'd be no job here for you, right?" Looking hard at the gunfighter, he added, "Then you wouldn't have to worry about your reputation. Nobody could say you left before he—"

"Nobody," Sandeen enunciated slowly, "will be sayin' nothin' except that Kane and me faced each other here . . . and that Kane died."

"But if he didn't come?" Katherine insisted.

"Then there'd be nothin' keepin' me in this hole of a town. But Kane's got a reputation to worry about, too." He smirked, then murmured, "He'll come."

"He'll come," Angus Mallory said forcefully, "and he'll stay long enough to see you dead, Sandeen. Tom Clancy was a good man, and I aim to see his killer set down cold."

"You have the backbone to try and do that yourself?" the gunfighter asked.

"That'll be enough, Sandeen!" Seth Garlath exploded. "From here on, gunfighters will shoot at gunfighters— nobody else! You got me?"

Angus Mallory nodded. "And when that's done, we can talk about havin' no Mallory gunfighter in town—but not before."

Katherine Mallory walked toward the door that led to the main room. She turned, and there was a look of determination on her face as she told her father, "Maybe . . . and maybe not."

David rose from his chair. He looked at his father, then at Angus Mallory. "You just won't budge, either of you. Well, somebody's got to try to stop this craziness."

"That gonna be you, boy?" Sandeen asked.

David looked at the gunman with narrowed eyes. "You never can tell."

Sandeen smiled. "Strong talk for a man without a gun."

David smiled back. "Maybe that's something else you never can tell about."

"David!" Seth Garlath warned.

But his son said nothing as he followed Katherine out the open doorway.

David caught up with Katherine outside the saloon. Her back was pressed against the wall just to the left of the swinging doors, and her fists were clenched so tight that the skin over her knuckles was bone white.

"David, let's leave. Let's just get into my buckboard and leave here and never look back. Now."

He took her in his arms and held her for a long moment. Then he stepped back from her, his hands still gripping her upper arms, his dark eyes looking intently into her blue ones. "You don't mean that. We've talked about it before, but you didn't mean it then, and you don't mean it now."

She sighed deeply and bowed her head, and her silken blond hair fell over her face. "Maybe this time I do," she said softly. "We've done all we can."

"I can't leave, Katherine. A man is dead because of the Garlaths, and as a Garlath, part of the responsibility is mine. I can't run from it."

"You didn't do anything to cause that!" she protested.

"I haven't done anything, period! But I'm still responsible. I'm a Garlath, and like your father says, blood is blood. I can't leave things as they are." His hands dropped to his sides, and he, too, sighed. "The damned thing is, I don't know what I *can* do!"

Stepping closer to the tall, dark young man, Katherine hugged him tightly. "I just had an idea. If we could stop Rado Kane from coming, if you and I could get to him and talk to him, maybe—"

He held her at arm's length and smiled at her. "That's

exactly what we'll do, Katherine! We *will* stop Kane from coming, one way or another. You get the buckboard and bring it here. There's something I need to get from my saddlebags."

She did not like the tone of his voice or the look in his eyes, and five minutes later, when he climbed into the buckboard and sat beside her, she did not like the pistol strapped to his leg.

Looking at him with wide questioning eyes, she asked, "David?"

He patted her hand reassuringly. "Don't worry. It's only for protection."

"You mind a question?" Rado Kane asked Juan Morales as they rode inside the stagecoach. The vehicle was five minutes out of Mohawk Station, moving eastward at a decent pace and flanked at a respectable distance on both sides by what might have been an honor guard of Mexican horsemen. Riding on top, aside from Walt Grader and Sam Loomis, were Lyman Whisters, who provided additional rifle support, and Judd Neep, his wrists and ankles tied securely. Inside the coach a glum-looking Gideon Cull sat next to the Mexican, across from Kane, Crystal Richmond, and Isabel Hallan.

"What is your question, Señor Kane?" Morales responded, his eyes on the Colt in Kane's right hand that was pointed directly at the bandit's ample stomach. It was uncocked, but the gunfighter's thumb rested meaningfully on the hammer.

"I'm wondering what you told your men. They certainly seem to have a look of confidence about them."

Morales's dark face brightened. "As well they should. Part of what I told them was that I had decided to guard the payroll from inside the coach itself. Such was the fear that I had inspired in you that you were forced to agree to my demand."

"They believed that?" Kane asked, astonished.

Morales's grin grew wider. "Why should they not? I

am their leader, and they know their leader as one who is most capable of inspiring fear in others as well as one who is always truthful."

Peering at the bandit, the gunfighter asked, "And what do you do when you have no payroll to show?"

"That, Señor Kane, is a separate problem. It is one I will have to think about, but I will produce a satisfactory answer. Believe me, I will."

Kane smiled. "Somehow I don't doubt that at all. What's the other part of what you told them?" He then grinned, adding, "And try to remember how always truthful you are."

Morales spread his hands. "It has to do with signals, signals of the hands. When a band of men like mine needs to talk together without sound, signals of the hands are used. I simply told them to watch for such signals from the coach windows."

"Signals to do what?"

The Mexican smiled. "There are many, many such signals, but I will give you a simple example. If my men see no signal at all from me for a long period of time, they are to make the conclusion that I have come to harm. After making that conclusion, they should at once attack the stagecoach and kill all of you gringos. Signals such as that."

"Useful," Kane commented, nodding and regarding the bandit with a degree of respect.

"*Mucho* useful," Morales agreed. "And in addition, this simple thing, this very simple thing of having them always looking for a signal from me is a very good reminder that, riding with them or not, I am still their leader and still in command. But now I have a question for you, Señor Kane."

"Sure."

"I am a man who wishes for little more than to continue to learn. For example, a man such as this man of the cloth here, he teaches me that different things are valuable to different people." Glancing at Gideon Cull, he told the preacher, "The way you forever grasp to yourself that bag of Bibles teaches me that the Holy Word of God can be, to some people, more precious than gold or money."

Looking up from his Bible, Cull brushed back a lank lock of his dark hair and scowled at the bandit. "God's words endureth. The baubles that common men hold of value are as nothing in the—"

"And you, Señor Kane," Morales interrupted, rudely dismissing the preacher, "you teach me that skill with a revolver can make one man much more valuable in a battle of guns than a small army of men not so skilled. I saw your every move yesterday, and I could not help but appreciate them."

"Some of your men might feel different," the gunfighter remarked dryly.

Morales laughed. "The dead ones feel nothing." Looking briefly at Cull, he told him, "My apologies, Reverend, but that is my opinion." Then, facing Kane again, he added, "The others, you are no doubt right about them. Especially Pico the Half Face."

"Odd name," Kane observed.

"Odd, yes. It is also recent. Pico is the man you shot from the door of the coach." The Mexican looked out of his window at the line of horsemen on his side of the coach and mused, "I do not see Pico. He must be riding on the other side. But, very clearly, the act of removing him from the stagecoach was a wonderful piece of movement and shooting. You will understand that Pico would not share my enthusiasm. In fact, he has asked for the pleasure of killing you personally if that becomes possible, and he wishes the process to be a very long one."

"You said you had a question."

Morales nodded, still enthusiastic. "That is true. I take it from your skill that you must be one who is a professional with the gun. Yes?"

Kane said nothing, his face tightening as he glanced swiftly at Crystal.

"I did not mean an offense," Morales gushed, "but

you should not be ashamed of such an occupation. I would give much to have your skills."

Again Kane said nothing. It was Crystal who broke the silence. "Mr. Kane learned his skills, as you call them, in the war. I don't think you would give much to have had *that* experience, Señor Morales."

Smiling, the bandit concurred. "There you are right, Señorita Richmond. Wars, they are for people who believe in things other than themselves. You are very right." He suddenly turned to Mrs. Hallan. "Señora, please, what *is* it you are doing with that wire?"

She halted the twirling movement. "I am making my own hand signals, Señor Morales. If I make the right one, I'm hoping some benevolent spirit from beyond will do something to make you shut your ever-speaking mouth." She watched him intently and smiled politely.

Morales seemed to consider the statement, then smiled back. "I learn from you, too, señora. Do you want to know what it is I learn?"

"Not especially."

"Nonetheless, I will tell you. From you I learn that, although the Reverend's God has put many beautiful colors on this earth, there are some ways you can combine them in clothing to make them look not so beautiful."

Mrs. Hallan still smiled. "Coming from the likes of you, I take that as a compliment."

Crystal laughed, which drew Morales's eyes toward her. "And I have learned also from you today, señorita. You have shown me that in this Arizona Territory there are women whose very visage is such that men would die for it. And if men would die for such beauty, they would surely pay much money for it. You, señorita, could well be worth far more than the payroll money that caused me to ride from the south."

"I'm not for sale," Crystal said icily, her hazel eyes boring into his face.

"No, of course you are not. Not at present, because

there is no one who may sell you. And I would not be a buyer. I, Juan Carlos Santiago Morales, do not ever buy. I steal. Then what I have stolen, I sell. This is, I will admit to you, a very simple philosophy, but simplicity is very much a desirable thing, on the whole. It is only when one contemplates life in the larger sense that things become complex."

"Life in the larger sense," Kane cut in, "includes death—and that, too, can be very simple." He flicked his glance from Morales to his Colt and then back again.

Morales flashed his toothy grin. "Let us hope that there will be much time and many places to experience before we taste that final simplicity." Turning to Cull, he suggested, "Perhaps, Reverend, you would say such a prayer for all of us—including my men who ride with us as well. What kind of leader would I be if I failed to include my men in such a matter?"

Saying nothing, the Reverend Gideon Cull looked away in disgust and turned his attention outside the coach window.

Chapter Nine

It was close to noon when the stage pulled up to a small swing station for a change of horses and a midday meal. The bandit "honor guard" had halted when the station had first come into view, and at a hand signal from Morales the men had abruptly ridden off to the south.

Walt Grader looked all around, shaking his head. "Not a damned one of them in sight," he observed.

"Out of sight, yes," Lyman Whisters agreed. "But we'd best not put them out of mind."

"Walt and me'll take care of the horses," Sam Loomis announced. Handing the peddler his sheath knife, the shotgunner asked, "How about you cuttin' our guest's legs free so you can walk him over to the barn? He needs to be outta the heat, and I need *him* outta my sight as much as them Mexicans."

Whisters cut through the four turns of rope that had tightly bound Judd Neep's ankles. Leaving Judd's wrists tied as they were, Whisters prodded him from the box with the barrel of what had been Bush's Winchester.

"There should be rope in the barn," Loomis offered. "You be sure to truss his feet up good again. We don't want him takin' a long walk outta here on us."

As Whisters marched Judd into the dilapidated barn, Grader called down to Rado Kane, "You want to put the Mexican out there in the barn, too?"

Kane had already spoken to the stationmaster. Returning to the stagecoach, he stood with his right hand resting on the butt of his holstered Colt. He glanced up at the driver and answered, "I'd feel a little safer having Morales where I can see him." Catching Crystal's eye as she started toward the one-room adobe building, he added, "Unless having him watch will bother you."

"Watch what?" she asked, clearly bewildered.

"Target practice," he answered. "The stationmaster has some shells for us. We'll practice directly after we eat."

Shaking her head forcefully, she declared, "I'm not sure I want—"

"It might be a wise choice," Isabel Hallan interrupted, "for you to do as Mr. Kane says, Miss Richmond." The elderly woman's voice was somewhat solemn.

"As for me, I always desire to observe," Morales remarked, grinning.

"Well, observe quietly," Kane retorted. "Otherwise we might decide to use you as the target."

"That also might be a wise choice," Mrs. Hallan commented dryly.

Inside the station building, lunch had already been set on the table by the stationmaster and his wife. Both in their mid-thirties, they were strong-looking people who appeared happy with their work and happy to greet the stage passengers. Crystal returned their greetings, then smiled meaningfully at Kane, but the gunfighter seemed to miss any meaning in her look.

"Eat up fast," he told her. "We won't be here all that long, and you've got some shooting to do."

"I'm still not sure I want to—"

"And I'm not sure that what you want is all that important," he cut in. "Right now your not knowing how to use a gun makes you a menace to every moving thing in Arizona—and there's more than enough menace out here already."

She laughed, then admitted, "I suppose I'm not in

any position to take offense at that. But I am pleased you
have such a strong sense of civic duty."

"Sit and eat," was all he said. And with a nod to Juan
Morales to do the same, Kane took a chair alongside the
Mexican at the table.

"Who's this?" the stationmaster asked Kane.

The bandit grinned. "I am Juan Carlos Santiago Morales," he said, removing his sombrero and bowing to the
stationmaster's wife.

"He's holding up the stage," Kane added.

Whisters came in, followed by Grader and Loomis.
"Where's the preacher?" the shotgunner asked the ped-
dler as the older man sat down at the table beside Mrs.
Hallan.

"He was heading out toward the privy," Whisters
said, pushing back his sleeves and reaching for the food.
"The man believes in doing first things first."

His pants around his ankles, what the Reverend Gideon Cull was mainly doing as he sat on the seat in the
privy was thinking, something he had done a great deal of
since Judd Neep had put in his unexpected appearance.
Damn the stupid boy! Cull thought angrily, knowing that
the others on the stage now viewed him with suspicion.
However, he also had been around enough to know that
preachers in this part of the country were generally looked
upon with less than favorable attitudes.

Still, if Judd said anything— Then Cull relaxed as he
realized that there was no reason why the youth should,
for Judd was not there to inform on the preacher, he was
after something—and Cull knew what Judd was after. As
he reflexively clutched his black satchel closer to his body,
Gideon Cull thought that the boy had tracked him like an
expert, which had surprised Cull, who had no idea the
young con man would have that kind of dogged determination, let alone the required skill.

Suddenly snickering to himself, Cull decided that
somebody as stupid as Judd would be just the sort of

person who would get his mind fixed on a single thing and keep it there. After all, that was what had made the boy so valuable to him in the first place. Night after night, Judd Neep had been able to tell the same story of his conversion with remarkable conviction, and night after night, silver and gold coins had gone into the Reverend Gideon Cull's hat. Yet their association had to end sometime, for Cull simply could not stand being with the boy.

The timely demise of the Widow Anderson had decided matters. Heading south immediately, riding as fast as he could, Cull had worried about the possibility of Judd following him. But it had been a remote worry most of the time, and it had grown more remote with every mile and hour. Once he had gotten on that stage, the concern had fled completely—until the youth's surprise appearance.

Dammit all! he groused to himself. The problem was that Judd *would* talk. Not right away perhaps, but if he actually had killed that old man at the way station . . . Even if he had not, he had definitely stolen a gun and a horse, and horse thieves were treated about the same as murderers. Cull was certain that if Judd thought he could save himself with the authorities, he would do or say anything he could think of.

The authorities—that was the key element. Judd must not be handed over to them. Cull decided that perhaps he could help the youth flee. If he engineered the boy's escape—and lined his pockets with a little money—then maybe Judd would be content to let Cull be. Then again, maybe not.

The preacher clenched his fists. He had to do something, and there would not be many opportunities to do much of anything. However, there was an opportunity right now, with everybody except himself and Judd inside eating.

A sardonic smile suddenly stole over Cull's hollow face, and he laughed aloud. "Eating! That's it! Yes," he murmured softly, "opportunity knocks just once, the Lord saith." His brow immediately furrowed in thought, and he mused, "Well, maybe it wasn't the Lord, but the thought was heaven-sent, anyway."

With that, he hitched up his pants and fastened his belt.

"The preacher is truly a man of God," Juan Morales remarked to Kane and Crystal as they watched Cull walk quickly toward the barn carrying a plate of beans, with the ever-present satchel tucked under his arm. "Not only does he care about the boy having food for the body, but he brings his Bibles to give him food for the soul as well."

The three of them stood out past the corral, well away from the horses and the station building. They had left the others inside relaxing out of the heat, and Grader had informed them that they had twenty minutes before he hitched up the new team.

"Perhaps he has qualities we haven't seen," Crystal suggested, referring to Cull. "After all, nobody else seemed to think about feeding the prisoner."

"I thought about it," Kane stated. "Briefly. I kind of wondered which would be better, starving or hanging." He turned and gave the bandit a questioning look. "What do you think, Morales?"

"That is not what I would call a good either-or choice," he replied, his tone serious for a change. "No, Señor Kane, I could think of many better ways of dying. There is simple old age, for example, or heart failure from too much activity in the arms of a beautiful woman. Even death by being shot would be a better way."

Kane gave the bandit a wry smile. "Well, I suggest you step away behind Miss Richmond or you may get your better way sooner than you want," he warned.

The gunfighter turned to Crystal and began schooling her in the basics of firearms, and Morales shook his head. "Señor Kane, I believe you are making a grave mistake in teaching a woman to use a gun. You never know whom she might decide to use it on."

Kane ignored the snide comment and continued his

instruction. "Now, the thing you want to hit, that's called a target."

"Really?" Crystal responded dryly, giving the gunfighter a polite smile. "I would have called it a hat."

Smirking, Kane retorted, "Very funny. Okay. Let's see what you can do."

"Well, look who's here!" Judd Neep exclaimed. "The right-hand man of the Lord himself!"

"Keep your voice down," Gideon Cull hissed. "I brought you something to eat." He studied the cuts and bruises on the youth's face for a long moment, then declared, "You don't look at all well, Judd."

"I can thank those Mexican bastards for that," the young man snarled.

"They beat you?"

Judd spat into the dirt, then mocked, "No, they gave me money when I told them I'd been converted to the Lord!"

"Why'd they beat you, boy?" the preacher asked, his deep-set eyes boring into the youth.

The young killer flung back his head, getting a tangled lock of straw-colored hair out of his eyes before taking a deep breath and replying, "They wanted to know why I was followin' the stagecoach, figurin' I knew of somethin' important it was carryin', else I wouldn't have been trackin' it like I was."

"And what did you tell them?" Cull asked, clutching the satchel tighter to his bony chest.

Judd's laugh was bitter. "Don't worry, I didn't tell them nothin'. That's why my face looks this way. I got marks in other places, too." He glared at the preacher, adding, "That's somethin' else I owe you for."

Shaking his head, Cull protested, "You misjudge me, boy."

"The hell I do! You ran out on me, Preacher—and I aim to make you pay for that."

Cull's face looked pained. "Judd boy, I didn't mean to

leave you behind. I had to leave in a hurry. I looked for
you, honest I did, but with the Widow Anderson dying
quicker than anyone expected, bless her departed soul—"

"That's bull! You expected she'd be dead exactly when
she was. All her jewels and money was gone from where
she had it hid, and she was lyin' in her bed from bein'
pillow smothered, just like them other women you done
in. I figure you left me around to take the blame . . . or
maybe the haul was so big this time you got downright
greedy and didn't see any need to share it. That sound
about right, preacher man?"

"Quite the contrary," Cull replied in a soothing voice.
"The Anderson woman had hardly anything worth taking.
I give you my word—"

"Never mind your word. I'm more interested in the
Word of the Lord—right there in that Bible satchel of
yours."

The preacher sighed and murmured, "Ah, Judd, it
pains me that you don't believe me."

Suddenly Judd seemed to notice the plate of food for
the first time. "That for me?"

Brightening, Cull answered, "It is, indeed. I thought
you might be hungry. You see, Judd, I really do care
about you."

"The hungry part's true, anyway," the youth rejoined
with a snort. He then displayed his bound wrists behind
his back, remarking, "Eatin' ain't gonna be easy, though,
unless you're plannin' on spoon feedin' me like I was some
baby."

Cull hesitated. "I'm not sure about untying that rope.
You might decide to use your hands for something more
violent than eating."

Judd shook his head. "All I'm thinkin' about right
now is that I'm starvin'—and that plate of beans looks
mighty damn good."

"You ought to be thinking about something else," the
preacher said, and then a gunshot from outside punctuated his statement. Judd jumped, but Cull smiled, reas-

suring him, "Target practice. But they won't be at it long.
Which brings me to my point—the thing you ought to be
thinking about."

"And what's that?"

Smiling benevolently, the preacher replied, "Escape,
Judd, my boy. I don't know if you killed that old man back
at Adonde or not, but you did steal a horse. Folks around
here don't take kindly to either thing. The way I see it, if
you're gonna escape the rope, you've got to do it before
these people give you over to the law. And they'll do that
in the first town this stage comes to that has a decent jail."

Judd's pale face became even paler. "Where's that?"
he asked hoarsely.

Cull shrugged. "I don't know. Might be all the way to
Tucson, but it might be a whole lot closer—maybe even
Gila Bend, which we'll be at before the sun goes down
today. The way I see it, escaping right now is your best
chance."

Judd looked at the preacher cautiously. "Why you
want to help me?"

Sighing, Cull breathed, "Judd, Judd, I've *always*
wanted to help you. Reflecting back, I can see how things
might look different to you, but I'm speaking the Lord's
own truth. Think about it, my boy. Now, be honest.
Haven't you gotten some things wrong before?"

"Well—"

"And isn't it God's truth," the preacher droned on,
"that lots of times when you think out something for
yourself—when you don't have me to help you think the
right thoughts—you come up with answers that aren't the
right ones? Isn't that God's very own truth?"

Judd's face took on a bemused expression. "Sometimes, maybe, but—"

"And, whenever I told you that something was the
right thing to do," Cull continued, "didn't it always turn
out that way? Always?"

"I—"

Clapping his hand on the youth's shoulder, Gideon

Cull announced, "We don't have much time to discuss it, Judd, boy. Now, turn around and let me start working on those knots."

The wooden post lay on its side, about thirty feet from where Crystal Richmond stood. Although her second shot had come closer than her first, it was still at least ten feet to the right of the target.

"It would help," she complained to Rado Kane, "if I were using a smaller gun, something lighter than this. I have to use both hands to hold this thing steady. If you insist that I learn to shoot a gun, why does it have to be one this big?"

"Because," Kane answered, "only one that big has any accuracy at a distance. You don't want a weapon that's only accurate if somebody you want to shoot is close enough to take it away from you."

"Mr. Kane," she responded impatiently, "what you don't seem to realize is that I don't want to shoot anybody at all. But for some reason, that fact keeps escaping you."

Kane nodded, his blue eyes twinkling. "You're right, it does. Now try it again, but this time straighten your arms more."

Brushing back her long black hair, Crystal frowned and squinted at the target.

"And open your eyes," the gunfighter commanded, "both of them. You can't shoot what you can't see!"

"Damn!" she said and fired. As the Colt jerked upward, there was an eruption of gravel twenty yards to the far side of the target.

"No," Kane said, sighing. "Keep your arms straighter. Like this."

He moved directly behind her and, reaching around her shoulders, firmly gripped her forearms. He pushed them forward, then his right hand moved to the weapon itself and aligned it with the target. As he did so, their bodies came together, and Crystal turned her face to his so that they were within an inch of touching.

"Is this more like it?" she asked softly.

"Er, yes," Kane said, quickly releasing her and step-ping back.

Juan Morales laughed with delight. "Ah, I now see that there *is* a benefit from teaching a woman—the right woman—gun shooting. You are to be commended, Señor Kane!"

Kane glowered at the bandit, barking, "And you, Morales, are to be quiet!"

Still laughing, Morales murmured placatingly, "Of course, Señor Kane, of course. I only wanted to make a correction to the statement I made earlier. Although, when all things are considered, it probably still is not wise to teach—"

Crystal's fourth shot obscured the rest of his state-ment. Gravel flew skyward several feet beyond and to the right of the target. Turning to Kane, she told him, "I think I could do better if you held my arms steady. Could you show me that again?"

Before Kane could respond, a gunshot rang out from the barn.

Kane whipped out his own Colt and pointed it at Morales. "Move it."

As they hurried toward the barn at a run, the door of the station building burst open. Sam Loomis and Lyman Whisters, followed closely by Walt Grader and the station-master, spilled out into the sunlight. Loomis was carrying his sawed-off shotgun, while the others were hefting pistols.

Behind them came the stationmaster's wife and Isabel Hallan. The older woman also was carrying a pistol, the same one she had used during the bandit attack.

"We heard the shot," Loomis told Kane as he caught up to him. "It sounded different from the ones from Miss Richmond's gun, so we came a-runnin'." Nodding toward the barn, he asked, "You sure it was from in there?"

"I'm sure," Kane replied. He cocked the hammer of his Colt as he entered the barn, then eased it forward again as his eyes adjusted to the shadowy light and he saw the two men clearly.

"I . . . he . . ." Cull said.

Judd Neep was lying on his right side, his untied arms and legs spread-eagled and motionless. His one visible eye and his mouth were wide open, as if he had received a final, shocking surprise. Certainly it had been final—the blood-soaked back of his shirt left no doubt about that.

The preacher's gun lay smoking on the dirt floor beside the metal food plate. A sizable portion of the beans that had been on the plate were now on the front of Cull's coat.

"He—he was free from the ropes when I got here," Cull explained. "I was trying to give him the beans when suddenly he made a grab for me, which is how I got splattered with food. God be praised that I had a chance to get my gun free."

Whisters knelt beside the dead youth and fingered the lengths of rope lying next to the corpse. "Odd as hell," he muttered. "These ropes had good and tight knots in them when I left him."

"Apparently not good enough and not tight enough," Grader remarked.

"The hell you say!" Whisters replied. "I tied those knots so tight I was afraid I was going to break the kid's skin!"

Loomis scratched his stubbled jaw. "Tight or loose, it's hard to see how he could've got out of 'em so fast. See there? He didn't slip through the wrist ropes. They're untied; not knotted at all." He looked at Cull questioningly.

"I have no idea how he did it," the preacher said huffily. "All I know is, he *did*. The ropes around his ankles looked as if they still were tied in place, and his hands were behind him when I came in. I had no idea he was free until he jumped at me."

Kane took his eyes from the body and stared hard at Cull. "Back first?"

"He—he turned away when he saw my gun," Cull quickly stated.

"Turned the other cheek, did he, Reverend?" the liquor peddler asked dryly.

Juan Morales hooted. "What a fine book is the Good Book! It provides an excellent quotation for every occasion!"

Kane's pale blue eyes regarded the Mexican coldly for a long moment. Finally gesturing with his Colt toward the open doorway, he told the bandit, "Get back outside—and watch your step, Morales. You wouldn't want to end up like the kid, now, would you? It would not be—how you say?—a pleasurable experience."

Chapter Ten

"Painted Rock comin' up!" Walt Grader called down to the passengers from the driver's seat on the box. "We water the horses and we water us! Next stop is Gila Bend!"

Rado Kane pushed back the leather curtain to see what was outside under the late afternoon sun. Aside from the tall saguaro cactuses and the gravelly sand of the Arizona desert, there was not much other than the way station, which looked so like the others that Painted Rock could easily have been their noontime stop or the one at Adonde the day before.

"Looks pleasant," Crystal observed, her voice sounding closer than it should have been. Turning his head sharply, Kane found that the young woman had moved to his seat and was also looking out his window. "I like the way each of these way stations we've stopped at seems to reflect the personalities of the station manager and his wife," she went on.

"You see a difference in them?" the gunfighter asked, astonished.

"Of course. The lettering of the signs, the curtains in the windows—you know, the type of material and the way they're hung—and a lot of other little things. You've not noticed?"

"No," he admitted.

Her hazel eyes gazed into his blue ones as she smiled

and noted, "But you *are* looking. Should I take that as a sign?"

"Nope. Looking is looking, that's all," he countered. And looking is not necessarily seeing, he thought to himself. Especially when there were things he did not want to see and things he did not want to feel. At least, not now. Certainly not now.

"You're not thinking about the possibility at all?" she prodded.

He looked at her for a long moment. "Right now, all I ought to be thinking about is Gila Bend."

Juan Morales stirred. Both he and Gideon Cull had been napping for most of the afternoon, and now he yawned and said sleepily, "Gila Bend. You have business there, Señor Kane?"

"*You* might have," Kane responded, "if there's law there."

The Mexican smiled. "I have been thinking about this for some time, and I have concluded that I do not wish to have much in the way of conversation with men of the law. They do not understand my philosophy of life, and there is little in the way of poetry in them . . . unlike me and you and Señorita Richmond and Señora Hallan—and even Señor Whisters. We are a different breed of people than the others. We live for the romance of life." He smiled, adding, "Would you not agree?"

"Speaking of romance," Kane said, ignoring both the question and Crystal's beaming face, "what happened to your romantic band of foolish men? Your riders seem to have disappeared after the last stop."

Morales nodded thoughtfully as he stroked his thick mustache. "I sent them away to meet me in another place. You know that I had this very big problem about not knowing what to tell them if I did not successfully get the payroll money, yes? Well, what I told them was that, if by the next station I did not give the hand signal for them to attack, they should go on ahead and wait for me to join them. If I did not give them the attack signal, that meant that I could best accomplish the task by myself." He suddenly sighed, then remarked, "The problem I have now is the payroll money. I think perhaps you were telling the truth, and it does not exist."

"What makes you finally believe it?" Kane asked.

"The actions of the stagecoach employees. When we stopped, everybody made certain that the horses were tended and made certain that I was watched and that the boy, Judd Neep, was taken care of—when he was alive, that is to say." He glanced meaningfully at the dozing Gideon Cull, then went on. "But the stagecoach, no one watched it. It would be very stupid not to have someone watch a stagecoach with payroll money on it, yes? There-fore, since no one here is very stupid, I must conclude that it is likely you told the truth, and that the money does not exist."

Kane regarded the bandit for a moment, then asked, "And how will you explain that to your men?"

The Mexican's face clouded, and his voice was more serious as he answered, "That is what I have to think about now, the next thing that I tell them."

The stage suddenly halted, and Sam Loomis's booted feet could be heard hitting the hard-packed earth outside the coach. The Reverend Cull jerked awake and, looking somewhat disoriented, asked, "Wh-where are we?"

"The paradise of heaven itself," Juan Morales replied. "Although it looks much like Arizona. May I carry your bag for you?"

"Don't touch that!" Cull snapped, then swiftly looked at Kane. "This man should be handcuffed!"

"This man is no threat to us, now that he understands we don't have any payroll," Kane stated. "Besides, he might need to give another hand signal if his men show up again. Let him carry your bag and earn his keep, Cull."

Cull reached for his satchel. "The Word of the Lord must not be defiled by the hands of heathen!"

Isabel Hallan barked out a laugh. "Odd," she commented. "I thought one of the things a preacher was supposed to do was bring the Word *to* the heathen."

Morales laughed. "Ah, Señora Hallan, you do not understand. To this preacher's mind, there are heathen, and there are *heathen*. The last kind of heathen are those like me, and we are not worth the time of any preacher. And do you know why? It is because we have no money to give to them in exchange for their preaching. That, I think, is the worst kind of sin there is, having no money to line the preacher's pocket."

Cull sneered at the bandit and countered, "Do not make light of the Lord's mission to those who—"

"Who," Morales interrupted, "shoot and kill young boys to whom they offer food in barns?"

His dark eyes burning like coals, Cull roared, "That was self-defense! Damn you, listen to me!"

But Morales ignored him and, opening the door, stepped out of the coach, then helped Mrs. Hallan down. Cull turned to Kane and Crystal, but they, too, had their backs to him, with Kane helping Crystal out the other door.

"It was self-defense!" Cull cried.

"Pretty effective, too," Kane said quietly from where he stood beside the open doorway. Pausing for effect, he finally added, "Of course, one gun against none is always pretty good odds." He then turned on his heel and left Cull sputtering to himself.

Entering the station house, Kane was surprised to find all eyes within looking at him. Crystal Richmond had been talking to the stationmaster and his wife—yet another couple, this one in their fifties—and she broke off her conversation and smiled knowingly at him.

Sam Loomis stood over a dark-haired young man and blond young woman who were seated at the lone table in the room. "That's Kane," the shotgunner said to the couple, pointing at the gunfighter.

Hearing his name, Kane examined the pair more closely and decided that neither of them seemed older than twenty. The young man abruptly stood up, revealing a tied-down holster containing a pearl-handled Colt.

"You're Rado Kane?" he asked.

Kane nodded. "I guess I should ask who's asking."

The young man's dark eyes were cool as he responded, "My name is David Garlath."

"And mine," said the young woman as she stood, "is Katherine Mallory. Does the name Mallory mean anything to you?"

"The name Angus Mallory does," the gunfighter replied, shrugging.

"I'm his daughter."

Smiling, Kane observed, "Angus Mallory is a lucky man."

Katherine cocked her head and studied Kane. "You don't look or act like a gunfighter," she finally said.

Sam Loomis laughed heartily, declaring, "You weren't at the right places to see what he looks or acts like, miss. The rest of us was. Take our word for it, Mr. Kane here is whatever he says he is. Maybe more."

Lyman Whisters stepped forward. "What Mr. Loomis is saying, Miss Mallory, is that all of us are extremely grateful and probably owe our lives to Mr. Kane's prowess with a gun." Gesturing with his chin at the Mexican, he added, "Except for Señor Morales here, since he was the one who tried to take those lives."

Morales doffed his sombrero and bowed. "Juan Carlos Santiago Morales, señorita, at your service," the bandit said with a flourish.

Katherine stared at the Mexican. "If, sir, you are truly at my service, then perhaps you can persuade Mr. Kane not to take this stagecoach any farther."

Kane shook his head in bewilderment. "The daughter of Angus Mallory wants me *not* to come to Gila Bend?"

Katherine's chilly response was barely polite. "That sums it up nicely, Mr. Kane."

Kane's pale blue eyes narrowed as he asked her,

"What about Jack Sandeen? Your father seemed to think I was needed because of Sandeen."

"Sandeen," David Garlath put in, "is employed by my father. If you don't come to Gila Bend, there's no reason for him to remain. My father will pay him off, and then he'll leave."

"Just like that," Kane stated.

David nodded, and a lock of his dark hair fell onto his forehead. "Yep. Just like that. Sandeen killed a man two days ago, an unarmed Mallory worker, and that's made everybody on both sides of this whole thing madder'n hell. Nobody will work in the mines until Sandeen is gone, but he won't run from a fight with you."

The gunfighter assessed the tall young man standing before him. "So you're asking me to run," he finally declared.

David flexed the fingers of his right hand. "Maybe what I'm doing is *telling* you to run."

"David, no!" Katherine cried. She stepped toward him, but the look in his eyes stopped her cold. "David, please! Don't be foolish!"

"Nothing's worked, Katherine," the youth responded. "Nothing that you or I have said or done has made any difference. Maybe I should have faced down Sandeen instead of Kane, seeing as how it was my father who hired him, but Kane is here now, and so am I."

"There's no quarrel between us, David Garlath," Kane muttered. "I don't want to fight you—and believe me, you don't want to fight me." But the gunfighter's body was taut and ready, and he could feel the familiar cold alertness taking control of his nerves and muscles.

"Rado!"

Crystal's voice pierced the icy barrier that had surrounded him. And then he felt her hand tighten on his left upper arm, and he suddenly realized that she had been there by his side all along.

"It wouldn't be running," she told him in a voice that

was earnest—as well as something more. "You can just quit. Right now, you can quit."

It was a bad choice of words. Kane turned on her, demanding, "Quit and do what? Manage a way station? You've yet to find me that good woman I need." He inhaled deeply, then added, "Besides, if you'll allow me to make a professional judgment, as admirable as their motives are, these two young people are wrong."

"Wrong about what?" David asked, bristling.

It was Sam Loomis who answered from behind him. "Wrong about thinkin' you're gonna to draw against Kane. You make a move toward that gun of yours, I'll blow your hand off your wrist." The warning was followed by the sound of two shotgun hammers clicking back noisily.

Kane's body relaxed and he nodded his thanks to the shotgun guard. Facing the young couple, he explained, "Miss Mallory, Mr. Garlath, what I meant by you being wrong is that Sandeen won't leave. Whether I show or not will make no difference."

"And why not?" Katherine asked coldly. "Do you know him personally?"

"No, but I know the type. He's killed someone already, an unarmed worker, you said. Well, the kind of man who'll do that isn't about to leave before he gets ready to. When you hire a shooter like Sandeen, you maybe hire somebody who decides to take things over . . . especially when there's nobody to stop him." He smiled crookedly, then added, "I'm the only somebody around who can do that."

"You certainly think a lot of yourself!" David exclaimed. "What makes you think we can't handle Sandeen ourselves?"

Kane smiled humorlessly. "Because you haven't. You said the men on both sides were mad as hell about the killing. Well, if that's the case, then why's Sandeen still around? Men who are mad as hell usually do something about what they're mad about—unless it involves a professional gunfighter. Especially a gunfighter of a particular kind—one who shoots down unarmed men. But I suspect there's a second reason why your idea wouldn't work."

"What's that?" Katherine asked.

"Your father, miss. He's lost a man to Sandeen. If I don't show, he'll just hunt himself up another gunfighter who will. In the meantime, nothing changes."

"But there shouldn't be this kind of war in the first place!" Katherine moaned. "The two men—my father and David's—used to be great friends. This whole thing has just grown by itself."

"Don't tell me," Kane commented. "Tell them— although judging by the way you both rode all the way out here to try and put an end to it, I'm sure you have. Plenty of times. But it *will* end, Miss Mallory. You two ride on back and tell both sides I'm coming in with the stage. There will be peace in Gila Bend, but the only way it'll happen is if I force it."

"Peace," Morales mused. "It is a fleeting thing. Only war is constant; it is the proper state of mankind."

"Nicely put," Lyman Whisters commented from across the room. "Who's that from, some Spanish philosopher?"

"It is possible," the bandit replied, giving the salesman an offhanded shrug. "It is also possible I just made it up. Perhaps I have not mentioned that I am also a poet."

Katherine and David spoke softly to each other for a moment. Then Katherine turned to Kane and told him, "I guess we don't have any choice but to let this whole thing play out."

Clearly agitated, David ruffled his thick dark hair and told the gunfighter, "I sure hope you can live with your decision—and yourself, Mr. Kane." He then took Katherine by the arm, guided her outside, and helped her into their buckboard.

Watching them go, Crystal felt a pang of fear, not for the young lovers but for Rado Kane. She looked up at him from her place at the table, where she had sat down with most of the other passengers and crew, wondering what was going through Kane's mind at the moment.

He obviously felt her gaze, for he looked down at her and asked, "You think I'm wrong, don't you?"

"I don't know," Crystal answered, her lovely face reflecting her troubled mind. She glanced briefly at Gideon Cull, who sat gloomily in a corner away from the others, and thought briefly about spiritual guidance, but then she quickly looked away.

Except for Morales, who had been allowed to visit the privy by himself, the travelers all sat quietly, in part reflecting on the upcoming incident and in part merely enjoying the respite from the ride. Mrs. Hallan abruptly took out her piano wire, turning it slowly and looking through her almost-closed eyes at each of the others in turn.

"Kane's not wrong, Miss Richmond," Sam Loomis stated, breaking the silence. "That feud between Mallory and Garlath has been goin' on for I don't know how long, and it ain't gonna end until somebody else ends it. Kane might just possibly be that somebody."

"You know Jack Sandeen?" Lyman Whisters asked the shotgun guard.

"Seen him once, from a distance. From what I seen, that was close enough. Mean-lookin' dude. Real mean lookin'."

Whisters nodded. "Hired guns are supposed to look mean."

"Rado doesn't!" Crystal exclaimed defensively.

Kane turned to her and scowled, but he was not able to maintain the expression. He, along with everyone at the table, laughed almost immediately.

"Well, now, I recall a time, Miss Richmond," Loomis interjected, "when you didn't think like that at all. As far back as yesterday mornin', in fact."

Crystal felt her face flush. "There were, um, things . . . things I didn't . . . realize yesterday morning, Mr. Loomis," the young woman said softly, looking down at her lap. Silence again fell over the room, and after a moment she looked up at Kane.

His eyes were on hers, and there was something in them that disturbed her. *No,* she thought *disturbed isn't the right word, exactly. Excited or thrilled is much, much closer.*

Kane shifted his eyes, abruptly breaking their connection as he focused on the mug of coffee he lifted to his lips. After a few moments he again looked at her, but when he did, there was a forced hardness in his expression.

Crystal was taken aback by the impact of his initial gaze, and she felt as though a hammer were beating into her heart. She tried to recapture the moment, replaying what it was that had passed between them, when Whisters broke the silence—and her concentration.

"You know, Kane," the peddler remarked, "a couple of times during the past two days you've mentioned the thought of giving up your present occupation. Might I suggest that the life of a salesman isn't all that bad—and that, from what I've seen, you might possess several of the personal traits required."

"Whisters . . ." There was a note of warning in Kane's voice.

"Of course, I wouldn't presume to press the matter," the liquor salesman continued. "Don't get involved with other people and their problems, that's what I always say. And it's a rule I never violate."

Walt Grader's eyebrows raised questioningly. "Never?"

Suddenly the sound of hoofbeats racing away from the way station brought everybody to their feet.

"What the hell—" Loomis shouted, charging toward the door, his sawed-off shotgun appearing in his hand as if by magic.

Grader reached the door first, yanking it open. "Son of a—" He left the rest unsaid.

Loomis lowered his weapon as Kane and Whisters flanked him. They all stood watching two riders beating hell for leather toward the west.

"There goes our sometimes poet," Whisters remarked.

"Good riddance, I say," Loomis muttered.

"The riddance is good," Kane agreed. "I'm not sure what else it may be."

"What *I'm* sure of," Grader declared, "is that we pull out in five minutes." Turning toward the others, the driver announced, "Any of you want to hit the privy, it's now or it's Gila Bend."

Everyone stepped outside, and while Grader and Loomis saw to the horses, Whisters, Isabel Hallen, and Cull took the privy suggestion seriously, leaving Kane and Crystal suddenly alone by the side of the coach. He took her arm gently and guided her to a place behind the rear boot where they could not be observed.

Clearing his throat, Kane began, "Crystal, I want to say— I mean, I told you a lot about myself last night. Well, maybe not a lot, but more than I've told most people. One thing I didn't mention was a woman."

"There's a woman?" she asked in a small voice, her hazel eyes studying his face intently.

"No. There isn't, and there hasn't been. I mean, nothing serious. A man who does what I do can't involve himself like that. It wouldn't be right. Not for the woman, who'd never know when I rode out if I'd ever ride back in, and not for me, either. Having a woman would do something . . ."

"Give you someone to care about?" she asked.

"Yes, something like that."

A gust of wind blew a wisp of her long black hair over her eyes. She reached up and tucked it behind her ear, then asked, "Having someone to care about, that's a bad thing?"

He looked at her, his face no longer hard. "When I faced Billy Nathan yesterday, I didn't have to think about anything but Billy Nathan. I didn't have to think about anybody caring a single bit about me possibly going down. When I face Jack Sandeen tonight, it has to be the same."

"Whether it's true or not?"

Rado's arms suddenly were around her. Their bodies

melted together as one for what seemed to Crystal an eternal moment. Then his hands were on her shoulders, and he gently but firmly held her away from him.

"You answered my question," she said softly, looking away. Tears had welled up in her eyes, and she did not want him to see them. Surprised by their presence, she did not want to take the time to think about why they were there—just that he not see them. But then she thought to herself, *I'm being a damned fool! Of course he sees them. He's not blind—no, not at all!*

She looked up at him, and to her surprise, Kane was smiling. "I guess that was kind of a strange answer. If I were Morales, I probably would have had a smarter one."

She wiped away her tears as discreetly as she could, responding with a small smile, "Well, smarter, maybe. But not better. Not better by a long shot."

It was close to seven-thirty when the stage pulled into Gila Bend, and Kane and Crystal looked out the window at the town. There were few stores and even fewer people to be seen.

"You were right," Crystal said to Kane. "It doesn't seem to be much of a town."

"The hotel's clean," Whisters remarked from the opposite seat. "That much I can vouch for—and I can vouch for the food there, too. Providing Mrs. Grogan still oversees the place, that is."

Crystal could see the bright white and red sign over the doorway that proclaimed the two-story building they had stopped across from to be the hotel. It was, in fact, the sole building on that side of the street. On the other side were two one-story buildings, one of which had no mark of identification, and while the second had no sign either, its batwing doors were advertisement enough. A cold shiver suddenly went down the young woman's spine.

"That's Hawk Brown's place," Whisters explained to the gunfighter, pointing at the saloon. "Hawk owns and runs it. He's also the town marshal—but not so's you'd notice it much."

"You mean he won't get in the way," Kane remarked dryly.

"Not intentionally. And if he does so by accident, he'll try like hell to get *out* of the way by the fastest route possible."

Kane nodded. "Anything else I should know?"

Whisters shook his head, the expression on his pudgy face deadly serious for a change. "You already know about the main players, except for the two mine foremen. I wouldn't exactly classify them as main players, but in any case, I can see you're about to meet them. That's them standing in front of the saloon."

It soon became apparent that the unmarked building the stage had halted in front of was the Concord Stagecoach Line station. As the passengers stepped down from the coach, Gideon Cull took off without a word toward the hotel. Whisters, Crystal, and Isabel Hallan stood watching Kane as he looked first up and down the street and then at the barn and corral behind the station.

"Quite a few horses," he noted to his fellow passengers. At least two dozen mounts were tied up to the hitch rails, and the majority of them were saddled.

"Never seen that many here before," Sam Loomis observed as he stepped down from his side of the box. His weathered face was screwed up in thought for a moment before he declared, "Guess some of the miners decided to come see the show." He looked at Kane quickly. "Sorry. I know you don't like that word."

"Don't make much of a difference," Grader pointed out as he began to open the rear boot so the passengers could get their baggage. "Whatever it is to you, Kane, to them it's a show. I don't reckon to miss it myself."

The two men Whisters had identified as the mine foremen approached the group, and the taller of the two stepped in front of Kane. "My name's Let Cutler. Are you the gunfighter?"

Kane nodded at the man.

"I work for Angus Mallory. He wants me to bring you to where he's waiting in the hotel lobby."

"Excuse me, Mr. Kane," said the second man. "I'm Clay Brock. My boss is Seth Garlath. He asked me to give you a message, too."

Kane looked at the man wordlessly.

"He said to tell you Jack Sandeen is waiting in the saloon."

Kane turned to the peddler. "What's the price of one bottle of your good stuff?"

Smiling, the salesman quipped, "For you? How about one the Mexicans broke?"

"The price seems reasonable," Kane replied, chuckling. "I'd like it now."

"Done." Whisters went to the rear boot and took his case from Grader, then opened it.

Turning to Crystal, Kane said, "I've a favor to ask." Then he looked at Mrs. Hallan. "Of both of you."

"What is it?" the older woman queried.

"First crack at a bath. I got a feeling you both are looking forward to having one."

Crystal blushed. "That sounds a bit personal, but you're right. Maybe I shouldn't have been thinking about things like that at a time like this, but—"

"I completely understand," he assured her, grinning. "It's all right. It's normal. And it would be normal for Whisters and me to hold back and allow you ladies to have first use of the tub. But, well, under the circumstances . . ."

"You're asking me"—she glanced at the older woman—"you're asking us if you can go first?" Crystal reiterated.

"Yes." He took the bottle Whisters gave him and nodded his thanks. "A man should be clean and relaxed when he faces another. I can't always manage it, but given the chance, I try."

"Well, of course!" Crystal said. "I mean, it's fine with me."

Mrs. Hallan shrugged. "Another hour or so won't make any difference to me, either."

"My thanks to both of you ladies." Kane then faced Brock. "Now, you tell your boss to tell Sandeen that he's going to have to wait. He's been waiting a long time, so he can wait a little longer." Turning to Cutler, the gunfighter told him, "In a few minutes I'll be checking in at the hotel, and I don't want to see either you or your boss there. Now that I've arranged a bath, I plan on getting straight to it, and after that I'll be resting a bit. I'll meet both Mallory and Garlath—and Sandeen—in the saloon in two hours. Tell them to be there promptly."

Pivoting, he went to help Crystal and Isabel with their bags. As he was setting them down on the street, a hand grasped his elbow.

Crystal was regarding him with fear-filled eyes. "What do I do for two hours?"

"I don't know, really I don't. I've never had anybody ask before."

"Kane . . . Rado . . ." Her voice was a whisper. "Before that, before you have to leave the hotel, can I . . . can we—"

Mrs. Hallan cleared her throat loudly. "If you'll excuse me, I'd best be seeing about my room." With a toss of her white-cropped head, she picked up her bag and walked briskly toward the hotel.

"Rado—" Crystal began again.

Kane shook his head. "A bath, some rest, and some of Whisters's finest. That's all I want for now. Later, perhaps, I—we—can maybe think about other things."

She moved to him, and for a moment Kane was unclear himself whether he would respond. But then, as her body began to tremble, his arms closed around her.

"Oh, God, I'm scared," she said in a tremulous whisper.

"Crystal . . ."

This time she pushed back from him, breaking his hold on her. "You're right. I know you're right. You can't think about—I had no right to say what I just said or to say anything else about how I—"

She breathed in deeply, then exhaled, and her body straightened as her hands smoothed her hair. Then she smiled. "Rado Kane, I want to thank you for the past two days. It's been an education, to say the very least. Two hours from now—or perhaps two and a half hours from now—if you have a mind to visit my room, I would welcome the opportunity to thank you properly."

She turned and walked toward the hotel. Not too fast, not too slow, but naturally and with dignity.

"That's quite a woman," Lyman Whisters mused appreciatively.

"She sure is."

"And she's right about the stage companies always looking for good—"

"Whisters!" Kane broke in, his voice cautioning. "Now is not the time!"

The salesman shook his head and said lightly, "Oh, I don't know. I'm the last person to interfere in the lives of others, but a man's gotta think about something while he's taking a bath and drinking a bottle of booze some Mexicans already destroyed, now, doesn't he?" He picked up his case and immediately started toward the hotel, leaving Kane to catch up with him.

"Speaking of Mexicans, that bunch is mighty familiar looking," Kane observed to Whisters and Loomis as they entered the hotel. He nodded toward a group of men in sombreros who were lounging near the front desk. No one was in attendance, leaving the gunfighter to presume that the clerk was seeing to the women.

Kane stepped over to the group and confronted one of them, a large, fat man whose sombrero had a string of black rosary beads for a hatband. "We seem to have misplaced your boss," he remarked to the man. "Where is he?"

"My boss?" the man replied guilelessly.

Kane rested his hand meaningfully on the butt of his

revolver, while Loomis thumbed back the hammer on one of his shotgun's barrels. The fat man's eyes widened.

"Ah, you must be speaking of Juan Morales."

"Correct. Where is he?"

"Where, *sí*, where? Morales, señor, he is like the wind. He is everywhere at once but nowhere in particular to be seen." He grinned.

"Great. Another poet," Kane muttered, turning to climb the stairs.

Chapter Eleven

"**W**ell, Hawk, my friend, I see business is booming." Lyman Whisters glanced quickly around the saloon, stroking his graying sandy mustache. Turning back to the bar, he lifted his glass in mock salute to the saloon owner, then took a swallow. The glass contained Scotch whiskey, served without charge from an unlabeled bottle.

The peddler then nudged his bowler to the back of his head and gazed around the room again. Not only was no chair in the place unoccupied, but little in the way of standing room was left at the bar or anywhere else. Loomis had elbowed enough space at the bar for himself, Grader, and Whisters, but the noise in the place was such that the liquor salesman almost had to shout for Hawk Brown to hear him across the polished mahogany counter.

"I have a full consignment of this heaven-sent distilled beverage with me," Whisters told Hawk, "and I suspect that you'll be wanting much more than the usual. My other customers along the route may have to be slighted, but with the stage having been attacked by bandits I shall no doubt be able to explain things."

Hawk frowned. "This ain't business as usual, Whisters, and you know it. 'Course, on the other hand, this week has put a lot of empty shelf space where there ought to be bottles. I'll figure up what I need when I get the chance." He then moved down the bar to refill some empty beer glasses.

"I notice the marshal ain't wearin' his badge," Grader remarked. "Or his gun."

Loomis tossed off his drink. "Maybe not, but he's got himself a persuader back there." He tugged on the butt of his own sawed-off shotgun, the barrel of which was thrust under his belt.

Whisters pivoted and leaned his back against the bar. "I'd been hoping for a little game of poker to while away the time, but no one seems to be playing."

"That's 'cause there's a bigger game of chance comin' up," the driver commented.

"You're probably right," Whisters said with a sigh. "In any case, it's much too noisy and crowded. I need concentration and elbow room when I play."

"I'll just bet you do," Loomis quipped.

The salesman reverted to a previous subject. "Speaking of guns, I don't see many."

Loomis looked around the saloon, then nodded. "Don't reckon that's a bad thing." Gesturing at the pistol in Whisters's belt, he commented, "I see you're carryin', though."

"I'm always carrying, Sam."

"Me and Walt, too," Loomis stated with a laugh. "No sense takin' any more chances than you have to."

"Speaking of taking chances, which one is Sandeen?" Whisters asked the shotgunner. "I don't see anybody who's as fearsome looking as he's made out to be."

"He's not here," said somebody to his left. Whisters turned to see Clay Brock, the Garlath foreman. "If he was, the place wouldn't be this loud, not by a long shot."

"Perhaps he's run out?"

Brock grunted. "Think again. If Mallory's man isn't in any hurry to get here, there's no reason Sandeen should be." The foreman took a sip of his beer, then asked Whisters, "This Rado Kane, you know him well?"

Whisters shrugged. "I never saw him before taking the stage with him from Yuma."

"Well, that's good, because that way you won't be losing a friend."

"Meaning?"

"Meaning you won't be seeing him again—not after tonight. From what I hear, he's no match for Sandeen. Kane shies from killing, Sandeen doesn't. Simple as that."

"Admittedly, that sounds simple enough," Whisters responded. He nodded at the crowd. "I take it that most of these men figure it the same way?"

"Sure, including the Mallory workers," Brock answered. "A couple of the fellas tried to lay some bets on the fight, and nobody would back Kane—nobody at all. Mind you, there isn't anybody here who wouldn't like to see Jack Sandeen fall tonight, but there also isn't anybody who figures he will."

Whisters smiled. He pulled a heavy-looking coin purse from the inside of his coat and looked at it. "Not having ever seen this Sandeen gentleman, I admit to being at a disadvantage. Nonetheless, Mr. Brock, I am in a wagering mood. How about yourself?"

"You—you want to bet on Kane?"

Whisters hefted the purse. "Yep. Until this—or takers—runs out."

Brock licked his lips. "I'll take five dollars of that." Addressing the room at large, he shouted over the noise, "We got us a betting gentleman here, boys!"

"Mr. Loomis," Whisters told the shotgun guard, "as one who holds the respect of all of us here—and who also holds a formidable weapon—would you consider serving temporarily as a banker? Fair compensation for your service, to my mind, would be, oh, shall we say, five percent of the winnings?"

As a mass movement of eager faces began toward the bar, Loomis shrugged. "Sounds fair to me, Mr. Whisters."

From the large second-floor window of her hotel room Crystal looked out onto the desert. Although she sat as still as a statue, her mind was in turmoil.

She had not seen Rado Kane since leaving him by the stagecoach. Whisters had brought her bags to her room, which was across the hall from his, and although he had a somewhat sympathetic look on his face, he had not said anything other than to announce that he figured she might have need of her things. What she wished she had told him then was she also might welcome a bottle of his whiskey. She rarely drank spirits, and when she had, she had moved from sober to a half-drunken state with remarkable rapidity. But that was precisely what she could use at the moment.

About half an hour after Crystal had gone to her room, the hotel owner had knocked to inform her that the bath was free. "That gunfighter acted as if he owns the place," Mary Grogan had complained. "Never mind that civilized ladies like yourself and Mrs. Hallan also have a need of the facilities, he just up and insisted that I draw the bathwater for him, just like he was Prince Albert or somethin'. Well, maybe if we're all lucky, them two gunfighters will be shootin' each other to death, and we'll be well rid of both of them."

Crystal had smiled weakly, saying nothing. After all, she knew absolutely nothing about this Jack Sandeen. If he was the type of killer that David Garlath and Katherine Mallory had said he was—and that Kane had confirmed he probably was—then she could understand how Mrs. Grogan might feel. But to assume that Kane was the same type of man . . .

She chided herself as she blankly stared out the window, not focusing on anything. Well, why should the hotel owner or anybody else not assume that gunfighters are gunfighters, and that all of them—

No, Crystal abruptly admonished herself. Rado Kane *was* different. She knew that in her heart. But she also knew that her heart was not thinking very straight all of a sudden, all of which added up to her really not knowing much at all.

Crystal sighed and pulled herself from the window, then walked across to the dresser. She stood there, nervously fingering the cameo she had unpinned from the suit she had been wearing. After having finally taken her bath, she had unpacked her clean traveling outfit—a tan-colored long skirt and a matching peplumed jacket that she wore over a white cotton lawn blouse—and hurriedly dressed, then brushed her long black hair dry.

Sighing again, she was just about to pin the cameo on her jacket when a knock sounded at her door, and she raced to it, her heart pounding. Pulling it open, she found herself staring expectantly at Isabel Hallan.

"I'm sorry to disappoint you," Mrs. Hallan said, her eyes carefully assessing Crystal. "Still, I sensed you wanted to talk with me."

The woman's smile was genuine, and Crystal returned it, although with difficulty. "Yes," she managed to murmur. "Please come in."

When they were seated—the young woman on the edge of the bed and the older woman in the lone chair in the room—Crystal asked, "What can you tell me? Do you know what will happen tonight?"

The smile instantly disappeared from Mrs. Hallan's face. "Knowing something and telling what I know can be two quite contrary things. For example, in Yuma I bought a ticket to Tucson, *knowing* that was where I was going. At the moment, however, I believe I won't be going there after all, at least not for a while, for if what I now *know* turns out the way I think it will, I'll be staying around here for a time."

"It's Rado I want to know about."

"I understand that. You also have questions about your own future . . . and you think that having some answers now might help you make the right choices, help you take the right actions."

"Yes," Crystal responded, her voice barely above a whisper.

"No. Definitely no," Isabel Hallan countered. "Using

the gift I have to help find metal in the ground is one thing. It's either there or it's not there. But when you're dealing with human beings—the man Bush at Adonde, for instance."

Crystal nodded. "You knew—"

"I *knew* only that he was in danger, and I sensed that he should be careful. But *telling* him that would have changed very little, or so I believe."

Confused, Crystal murmured, "I don't understand."

Mrs. Hallan smiled her sphinxlike smile. "There's a story from India that people like me use to help understand it ourselves. A man was told by a very skilled seer to watch out for tigers on his way back to his village, for the seer had had a very clear vision of the man being killed by a tiger. On the way home the man cautiously approached every tree he came upon and every bush to either side of the road, to be sure there was no tiger lurking behind it. So much did he focus his concentration on seeking out the places where a tiger might be hiding that he was careless as to where his feet were taking him. He fell into a half-covered pit that the villagers had dug to trap animals. His tiger was there, waiting for him."

Crystal's eyes filled with tears. "Then there's nothing you can tell me, except that the future is what it will be . . . and there is nothing I can do about it."

The older woman got up and walked to the bed, taking Crystal's hands in hers. "No, I'm not saying that at all. I'm saying that having some old biddy like me give you warnings or advise you on courses of action isn't worth very much. Yes, the future—your future—is very much what it will be. But you are the one most responsible for that future, and you are the one who can affect it most. Whatever you want to happen, do your damnedest to make it happen!"

Isabel Hallan smiled reassuringly at Crystal, then left, and the young woman once again went to the window and looked out, staring blankly at nothing. There was nothing to see from her window anyway except the desert and its

sentinel saguaros. She could not see the street or the
saloon from there, as much as she wanted to. Perhaps it
was a small desire, in Mrs. Hallan's terms, but it was
something she wanted.

Starting, she wheeled around. Lyman Whisters's room
was on the other side of the hall. Perhaps from there . . .

Crystal dashed across the hallway to the peddler's
room and knocked softly. There was no answer. She knocked
again, this time louder, but still there was no response.
She tried the doorknob and, finding the door unlocked,
opened it slightly. "Mr. Whisters?" she called. When it
was obvious that the room was unoccupied, she went
inside. "I hope you won't mind my borrowing your room
for a while," she said aloud. "Or actually, just your window." Crossing to the window, she decided that the salesman would not mind, especially since he undoubtedly
would not be back until after—

She shuddered and thought fleetingly about looking
for a bottle of something in the room, then saw that in fact
a bottle of that very something sat square in the middle of
the small bedside table. Giving her head a firm shake, she
moved the hard wooden chair in front of the window,
which gave her a command of the street and the buildings
across the way, and sat.

Command, she thought ruefully. *How ironic! I've got
command of nothing at all—at least not in the important
sense, not the way Mrs. Hallan had been talking.* Then
Crystal saw the older woman herself down on the street,
crossing toward the saloon, no doubt wanting to see with
her own eyes if things worked out the way she "knew"
they would.

Undoubtedly, too, Whisters had already made the
same crossing, and she assumed Grader and Loomis were
already inside the saloon as well. Where else would they
be? That was where the beer and whiskey were, and that
was where the show was going to be. Then Crystal saw the
sturdy figure of Mrs. Grogan head into the saloon, and she
caught herself beginning to smile. Probably the hotel owner

was seeing for herself which one of her boarders would not be returning to his room tonight.

Crystal immediately chided herself for her cynicism. After all, why would Mary Grogan or anyone else in and around Gila Bend want to miss the biggest event the town had probably ever seen? Only she herself was going to miss it—and, yes, the Reverend Cull, too. She had heard him in the room next to hers across the hall, probably still sulking about the way he had been treated by his fellow travelers after he had shot . . .

She found herself suddenly wondering if that was all there was out here in Arizona Territory—shootings and killings. But she knew—or at least part of her did—that there *was* more. Moses and Sally Elkins and the other station people had been genuine in their tenderness for each other and their concern for their passengers. And David Garlath and Katherine Mallory had been obviously distressed about what was going to happen tonight and sincere in their efforts to turn Rado Kane back and prevent bloodshed. They also were obviously in love. And Isabel Hallan, wherever her mind might be, had her heart in the right place for having come and talked to Crystal earlier.

Walt Grader, Sam Loomis, and Lyman Whisters, too—these were good and honest and hard-working men. Men who could be tough if there was a need to be tough, certainly, but men whose instincts and ethics were the right ones. And Rado Kane . . .

Precisely as his name entered her conscious thought, the man himself stepped out onto the street below her. He turned abruptly and faced the hotel, gazing up at the windows that looked out on the street. She inhaled sharply, pulling herself back from the window, not wanting him to see her, fearing she would break his concentration.

The light spilling from the windows illuminated him quite clearly. He was dressed in fresh clothing: white shirt with a black string tie, black jacket, and black pants. The black plainsman's hat was the same one Crystal had put two bullet holes in, but it was clean and looked almost freshly blocked. His face was now shaved, causing his chiseled features to be better defined. She had thought him handsome before, but she found this confirmation startling.

Her gaze fell to his right leg and the gun that was strapped to it. Her eyes closed. When they opened, she was watching his back as he headed across the street toward the saloon. Then she noticed the canvas bag he held in his left hand and wondered what it contained. But the thought was a brief one, and then her mind was filled with wondering if she would ever again see Rado Kane alive.

Kane had just pushed halfway through the batwing doors of the saloon when the door to Whisters's room flew open with a bang. Gasping, Crystal turned to find herself facing a pistol barrel.

"*Buenas noches, Señorita Richmond!*" Juan Morales exclaimed, and the bandit's grin was wider than Crystal had ever seen it. "You will be so kind as to accompany me quietly and quickly back to your room, for I have much to accomplish this night."

Standing shakily, Crystal's heart began to pound. She knew the Mexican was a man who would not hesitate to use that gun—if not to shoot her, then to club her into unconsciousness. Resisting him would get her nowhere, she knew, and so she reluctantly complied as he marched her back to her own room.

When they were safely inside, he laughed softly and told her, "I always suspected that you are as smart as you are beautiful, Señorita Richmond. Now you have confirmed that opinion for me." He then pulled a bandanna from his pocket and tied it around her mouth, gagging her with it. When he was finished, he remarked, "The thing about a gunfight like this one, Señorita Richmond, is just about everybody in town has gone to see it—which leaves men like me opportunity for profitable business."

Next Morales produced a length of rope from under

his gun belt and lashed Crystal's wrists together in front of her, then shoved her roughly onto her bed. After taking a swig from the whiskey bottle he had grabbed while in Whisters's room, he placed it on the table next to the bed. Then he extracted another piece of rope for the young woman's feet.

"Kindly put your ankles together, señorita," he instructed.

The foul-tasting bandanna that tightly gagged her mouth stopped any verbal defiance Crystal might have shown, but her eyes flashed with anger as her legs stayed separated.

"On the other hand," Morales said hoarsely, "perhaps I should not be so—as you say—hasty." Drawing his revolver, he cocked it and pointed it at her head while his left hand lightly caressed her calf. "Perhaps I will tie your legs together after taking advantage of the fact they are *not* together, *sí*?"

She shuddered and snapped her legs tightly together.

Morales sighed. "You are right. There is simply not enough time for such things right now." He swiftly looped the rope around her ankles twice and tied the ends in firm double knots.

Looking at her lustfully, the bandit told her in a thick voice, "It is a pity that I have so much to do—and one cannot know how long it will take one gunfighter to kill another and afterward for the celebration in the saloon to continue. But there will be another time when I *will* have the time. You have the solemn word of Juan Carlos Santiago Morales on that."

He took another swig from the bottle. "You know what is amusing, Señorita Richmond? I and my men come up from the south to take payroll money from the stagecoach. That is a business that has many dangers, as you saw yesterday. And yet, when it turns out that there is no payroll money—and I truly believe that is the truth of things—I find that I will be gaining much more in other goods. These will far more than—how you say?—compensate

for the missing payroll money and, even better, there are
no dangers in gaining them."

He smiled at her and grinned lasciviously. "You are,
in my opinion, a prize piece of goods. I know many men
to the south who will pay handsomely to partake of your
charms." Laughing, he added, "And to think that Señor
Kane could have had them for nothing! I had the eyes to
see that, even as he did not. Truly he is a foolish man, this
Rado Kane. Perhaps he will understand that, after he is
done with the affairs of the gun tonight—if, of course, he
is still alive then."

Walking to the window, the Mexican stepped out
onto the low-railed catwalk that ran the length of the rear
of the building. He waved down to his group of a dozen
mounted men below who were ringing an open wagon, in
the back of which were three large canvas sacks. One of
the sacks was empty and draped over the back of the
wagon, while the other two were filled, their ends tied
with ropes.

He turned back to Crystal. "Now, señorita, there is
one more bit of treasure hunting I must do before we
depart. I will be gone for only a few *momentos*," he added
in a low, menacing tone, "and I advise you to be very,
very quiet, for if you are not, my men have instructions to
come and kill you."

And then he was gone.

Crystal felt herself beginning to panic, then took hold
of herself. For the moment she was alone, but Morales
would be back, and how soon, there was no way to tell.
No, now was neither the time to panic nor the time to just
lie here on the bed in submission. Now was the time for
trying to take that command she had admonished herself
about just a few minutes earlier.

No! she shouted to herself. *Not try, but do!*

She braced herself for the collision with the bare
wooden floor and rolled off the bed. Her knees and elbows
protested in pain and continued to plead with her as she
used them to awkwardly make her way across the room.

She vaguely remembered playing a game like this—or was it some kind of race?—when she was a child. Well, she was in a race, all right, but it was against time.

Her suitcases were against the wall to the left of the door. *Damn!* she scolded herself. *Why was I in such a hurry to refasten them after dressing earlier? Damn, damn, damn!*

Chapter Twelve

The loud talk and laughter stopped as if noise itself had suddenly been outlawed the instant Rado Kane stepped through the swinging doors. Standing just beyond them, his gaze traversed the smoke-filled room before him.

The saloon was jammed. Not a single chair was empty, and not an inch of space along the three walls and the bar to his right was unoccupied. Glancing at the man behind the bar, Kane was certain that he had to be Hawk Brown—and judging from the barkeep's beaklike nose, there was no doubt how he had received his nickname.

Walt Grader and Lyman Whisters stood at opposite ends of the bar, and Kane registered the fact that Sam Loomis, his shotgun loose in his belt, stood with his back pressed against the far wall. The gunfighter was sure that the three men had strategically placed themselves to make sure the fight they anticipated did not get any unwanted outside interference. *Interesting*, Kane thought to himself. *Nobody's ever covered my back for me before.*

It took no more than thirty seconds for him to scan the entire room. He recognized the two mine foremen, as well as the woman who ran the hotel, who was sharing a table with Isabel Hallan. But he saw no one who could be Jack Sandeen, or the two men who had employed the gunfighters who were scheduled to perform tonight—at least not until the door on the far wall opened and three men stepped from a back room. These were the three he had come to meet, there was no doubt about it. And there was no doubt about which of them was Sandeen.

Garlath's gunfighter took a position at the far end of the bar, about six feet away from where Whisters stood. The man said nothing, merely smiling sardonically in a way that told Kane a lot about him. This was no Billy Nathan. This was a professional shooter who had looked at death many times and had always stared it down.

This also was no Calvin Dunny. No thoughts of last gunfights were in this man's head. Here was a cold-blooded killer who would keep killing until a bullet from somebody else's gun sent him to a cemetery somewhere.

Here?

Out of the corner of his eye Kane saw Mrs. Hallan's piano wire slowly twirling. Did she know the answer to his question? He shook off the thought. He would know soon enough, as would everybody else.

The larger of the two men flanking Sandeen, his weatherbeaten face as red as his bushy hair, moved directly to Kane. "It's about time! Where the hell've you been?"

"You know where I've been," Kane answered quietly. "You're Angus Mallory?"

"Damned right I am, and that's Garlath!" He stabbed a forefinger at the smaller man, then used the thumb of the same hand to indicate Jack Sandeen. "And that's his gunfighter. He's the man I want dead. That's what you've been hired for. And after you kill him, you can ask Garlath what he's done with my daughter!"

"I've been telling you, Mallory, I haven't done anything with her!" Seth Garlath countered. "I don't fight my battles with women!"

"Your boy took her, then. He hasn't been around either."

"I saw them earlier today," Kane told them calmly.

Both men stared at him, openmouthed.

"They met the stage and tried to talk me out of coming here," he explained. "Maybe they both said the hell with you and your fighting and went off on their own."

Mallory shook his head. "Katherine wouldn't just take off without sayin' somethin'! No, wherever she is, David Garlath took her there." He stabbed his finger at Seth Garlath again, snarling, "Same as *you* takin' her! Blood is blood!"

"Blood," Kane repeated evenly. "You gentlemen seem very eager to see some shed."

"You can believe that," Mallory confirmed.

Garlath nodded. "The sooner the better."

"It's good you agree on something," Kane quipped. "Now all that's left is to see if you're as good as your words."

He dropped his canvas satchel onto the floor in front of the feuding men and opened it up. Inside were a pair of gun belts, and Kane took them out, handing one to each of the mineowners. "Strap these on, both of you."

Both of them took a step backward, staring at the gunfighter as if he had lost his mind. "What is this, Kane?" Mallory finally demanded.

"It's what it looks like. Your argument ends tonight. The only way it's going to end is if one of *you* is dead, not one of your paid guns." And suddenly Kane's hand was filled with his own weapon. He looked at Sandeen, who merely grinned his bone-chilling smile. Then Kane looked back to the mineowners.

"I said strap them on," he growled. "Now!"

"This isn't why I hired you!" Mallory blustered.

"I suppose not," Kane remarked.

Seth Garlath turned to his gunfighter. "Sandeen!" he shouted.

Sandeen shrugged. "It's his cards right now. Frankly, I'm a mite curious to see how he plays them."

"Go ahead," Mary Grogan yelled. "Go ahead, you two old fools! You both like guns and killin' so damned much, you go ahead and do what he says!"

"Yeah," somebody else called, "put an end to it, like the gunfighter says."

"Damn right!" came a voice from the back of the room. "Tom Clancy would sure be liking to see that from wherever he is right now!"

The room broke out into mocking shouts and catcalls. There had been a lot of drinking going on for two days among many of the men in the room, and here was a bit of entertainment that had been unexpected, though it was something everybody wanted to see.

"All right," Garlath spat. He reached down toward the canvas bag. An instant later Mallory's hands were there, too, and the room fell quiet again as the two men quickly strapped on the gun belts.

"This will be a fair fight," Kane said. "You won't touch those guns until I tell you. Either of you tries, I drop him dead. Understood?"

Both men glowered at Kane as he directed them to opposite ends of the room, parallel to the bar. As they moved, so did many others, who scurried to get out of what they considered to be bullet range.

When the room was once again silent, Kane holstered his Colt. Keeping his eyes on Sandeen, he told the opponents, "You may fire when ready, gentlemen."

Both men went for their guns, awkwardly pulling them from their holsters. Mallory's gun went off first, but the bullet went down into the floor two feet in front of his own right boot. Garlath's first shot ricocheted off a brass spittoon at his end of the bar. With cries of pandemonium, everyone else in the saloon began diving for cover behind the bar and hastily overturned tables and chairs.

Kane and Sandeen stood their ground as each of their employers wildly fired his remaining five shots. Glasses behind the bar shattered, and splinters of wood flew from tabletops. When it was over, Seth Garlath was sitting on the floor with a bullet in his left thigh, while a bloodstain was growing on Angus Mallory's shirt at his left shoulder.

"You bastard!" Mallory shouted.

"Me? You tried to *kill* me, you redheaded son of a—"

"Gentlemen," Kane broke in. "You've still settled nothing. Despite your excellent attempts at marksmanship, you're both still alive. I've plenty more bullets in the bag. Shall we reload?"

The faces of both men went white with fear, and it was clear they had thought the ordeal was over with the emptying of their guns. But now this meddling outsider was forcing them to continue—probably until one of them was actually dead.

"This is stupid!" Mallory bellowed. He belligerently threw his gun down on the floor.

"*You* are stupid!" Garlath shouted. "You're the one who hired this man!"

"And you're a swindlin'—"

"Reload," Kane interjected loudly.

They stared at him. Seth Garlath's weapon then dropped to the floor. "No," he said sullenly.

"No," Mallory echoed.

"Then the war's over between you?"

The two men glared at each other in silence. Mallory broke it, muttering, "The shootin' part is."

"Garlath?" Kane prodded.

The gray-haired man nodded his agreement.

Shrugging, the gunfighter observed, "Then it looks as if my services are no longer needed—nor are Mr. Sandeen's. But, of course, he should hear that directly from you, Mr. Garlath."

Turning to Jack Sandeen, Garlath grumbled, "Directly from me, you're fired."

Every eye in the saloon was on the scarred, twisted face of Garlath's gunfighter. Jack Sandeen's own eyes narrowed as he looked at his boss and then directed his attention to Kane. "That was very clever, Mr. Rado Kane," the shooter said in his hoarse whisper. "I guess what I heard about you is true—and maybe what you heard about me is true, too."

Kane stared back. "I can't recall hearing anything about you. That is, anything except that you like to draw on miners who can't defend themselves with a gun."

Sandeen's lip twitched. "I'm faster than you, you know," he challenged.

Kane shrugged, his blue eyes not wavering from Sandeen's black glare. "I'm willing to let that statement stand."

"Figured you might be, but I'm not."

"We can still both walk away from this, Sandeen. The war's over. Nobody gains by us drawing against each other now."

Sandeen pulled tight the glove on his right hand. "You're wrong there, Rado Kane. *I'll* gain. I'll gain by bein' known as the man who took you down. I'm callin' you, Kane. *Now!*"

Both men went for their guns. Only one weapon fired. In rapid succession three bullets from Kane's Colt tore into Sandeen's chest. His lifeless body took down two empty tables before slamming forward onto the floor.

It was Sam Loomis who broke the hushed, stunned silence. "No wounded shoulder and smashed hand for this one, eh, Kane?"

Pulling three cartridges from his belt and reloading his pistol, Kane smiled tautly. "Think that would've stopped this one?"

"I doubt it."

"I doubted it, too."

A distant gunshot suddenly punctuated his statement, and everyone headed toward the batwing doors.

"That came from the hotel," Hawk Brown stated.

"Crystal!" Kane shouted, then pushed through the doors at a run.

In the room next to Crystal's the Reverend Gideon Cull's head snapped up as the succession of gunshots from across the street interrupted his thoughts. He was seated on his bed, fully dressed, his black satchel resting open on his knees. Within the bag was an assortment of Bibles, as well as Cull's pistol.

He had been sitting in that same position ever since

he had been shown to his room two hours earlier by the woman who owned the hotel. The preacher had neither bathed nor changed his clothes, bothered not at all by the discomfort of three days' growth of beard and the dirt of the road. Such matters were unimportant, especially given the decisions he had to make before morning.

He had been thinking about his predicament most of the day. Judd Neep was dead now, but the boy still could be dangerous to him. It was possible that what little there was in the way of law in these parts would be satisfied that a killer—or horse thief—had gotten himself killed, and that was that. Even though the stagecoach employees and passengers might be suspicious, there was no proof that things had not happened just the way Cull had said—and there was nothing to tie Judd Neep and Gideon Cull together. So what if Judd had stolen his horse? That meant nothing other than the horse was at the Adonde station, and Judd had stolen it. It could have been anybody's horse.

But it also was possible that someone in authority might want to know more about Judd Neep, including where he had come from. If that someone wanted to know bad enough, Judd might be traced back to where there *was* a connection with Cull—and a connection, too, to the possibly suspicious deaths of several widow women.

It was clearly decision time, yet the choice was unclear. Should he continue on the stage to Tucson in the morning? Or should he alter his original plan and, instead of turning south, switch to another line north to Phoenix and beyond? Both courses of action had their advantages and their disadvantages.

There was, for example, the Hallan woman. She had made her fortunes, she had said. She might prove a little more difficult to get close to, unlike some of the widows he had known previously, but if he turned up his charm on the stage to Tucson . . .

No. There was something about the woman and the way she looked at him. She might prove to be very dangerous herself.

He sighed, still uncertain as to his decision. On one hand, changing his travel plans might invite further suspicion if anybody continued to care about him. On the other hand—

"Shhhh!"

Looking up, Gideon Cull was shocked to see the face and gun of Juan Morales coming halfway through the window.

"Please make no sound, Señor Cull, and make no movement, either—other than to slowly stand and bring me that sack of Holy Books."

Three shots sounded from the direction of the saloon. Morales blinked, then frowned.

"You will hurry, please."

"My . . . my Bibles? Why would you—"

"Do not waste my time, señor," the bandit said coldly. "The boy Judd Neep did have some things to tell me when he was questioned, for we questioned him very hard. I have not felt ready to share with anyone what he said, but I felt I could share it with you now. The bag, *por favor!*"

Cull stood slowly, as he had been told. Grasping the bag with his left hand, his right moved swiftly inside. But the barrel of his pistol had not yet cleared the bag when a slug from Morales's revolver thudded into the preacher's forehead. The Reverend Gideon Cull was dead before he began to fall to the floor.

Moving to the body in two strides, Morales ripped the bag from the preacher's lifeless hand. "You should have listened, Señor Reverend," the Mexican muttered as he holstered his weapon. "Warnings from such a man as myself should never be taken lightly."

Stepping back out on the catwalk, the bandit considered throwing the bag down, then shook his head. Trustworthy his men might be, but one's trust is always best placed in oneself. "One more moment, *muchachos!*" he called down in a loud whisper. Then he took a few steps along the catwalk and leapt through the open window into Crystal Richmond's room, immediately drawing his gun.

"What have we here?" Morales asked, his voice mocking. "Trying to leave me so soon?"

In the darkened room he could not make her out clearly, but he could see well enough to determine that she was on her knees and elbows and had almost reached the door.

"No, señorita," the Mexican said with a sigh, "you do not get away so easily. I hope you do not mind being carried like a sack of grain to the outside of the window, but I will try to be very gentle. My men below will catch—"

A series of shots abruptly sounded from below in the hotel lobby. One of them was much louder than the rest—a shotgun blast. As the noise of the gunfire continued, it was joined by the pounding of boots rushing up the staircase.

"Ah, my men create a diversion," Morales said quickly, "but the diversion may not be entirely successful." He cocked his revolver. "Perhaps I shall have to create my own diversion. Tell me, señorita, who will be first through the door? Señor Rado Kane?"

Hurrying from the saloon, Kane, followed by Loomis and Whisters, had dashed across the street, into the hotel, and through the lobby. He was about to climb the stairs when from behind the hotel desk a sombrero shot up. Beneath the hat was a fat, dark face—as well as a filled gun hand. At the same time, two other Mexicans, their guns drawn, rushed in from the dining room.

Kane got off a shot at the man at the desk, then flattened himself on the stairs as a bullet thudded into the wall behind him. A second bullet then smacked into the railing above his head. He was about to squeeze off another shot of his own when an explosion sounded from the door, and the man behind the counter went down with a face full of blood from the blast of Sam Loomis's shotgun. Black beads from a rosary peppered the far wall.

"Watch out, Whisters!" Loomis warned as he ran into the lobby. "To your right!"

But even before the shotgunner had completed the warning, Kane's redirected Colt took down one of the two men there. Then Sam Loomis's second charge blew the other bandit back into the dining room.

Falling flat to the floor, Loomis and Whisters watched for more targets while covering Rado Kane's back. Taking advantage of their cover, Kane rose and again started up the stairs. He was scanning the lobby below him when a hammer click from the top of the stairs announced that that was where he should have been looking. But before he even had his adversary in full view, the gunfighter aimed his pistol and fired.

The man at the top of the stairs wore a white bandage that covered the lower left side of his face, identifying him as Pico the Half Face. The half of his face that was visible had formed into a smile as he had lowered his gun barrel toward Kane, but the smile had frozen in place as Kane's bullet tore into the Mexican's groin. His eyes bugged out in terror, and a scream of pain tore through his throat. It was cut short as a second shot from Kane's Colt thudded into Pico's chest. The bandit reeled to his left, then fell onto the railing with full force. It gave way with a splintering protest, and it and the dead man plummeted downward and crashed to the lobby floor.

"We're behind you!" Whisters shouted as Kane reached the top of the stairs.

Kane paused at the door to Crystal's room and looked back. Whisters positioned himself in front of Gideon Cull's door, his cocked pistol at the ready, while Sam Loomis, quietly dropping two new shells into his shotgun, took a stand in front of Whisters's room. Both men looked at Kane and waited in silence.

Kane made a fist of his left hand, then straightened three fingers, nodding to the other men. They nodded back. Then he made a fist again and slowly released first the index finger—*one*—then the finger next to it—*two*—and finally the third—*three*.

The three doors crashed inward at the same instant.

It took several seconds for Kane's eyes to adjust to the darkness of the room interior, but even before they had, he could make out the figure of the man wearing the sombrero directly outside the window, as well as the glint of metal at the man's midsection—an aimed gun. Kane had the fleeting thought that standing silhouetted in the open doorway as he was made him a perfect target, but before the thought was even complete, a gun roared from within the room. He reflexively stiffened, waiting for the impact.

There was none.

Instead, the man at the window cried out in a mixture of surprise and pain, and his revolver slipped from his fingers and dropped to the wooden floor inside the room. Surprised himself, Kane looked toward his right on the floor, the direction that the shot had come from.

His eyes now fully adjusted, Kane saw a tied and gagged Crystal Richmond holding Billy Nathan's smoking Colt in her two bound hands. At the window, Juan Morales, his eyes widened in disbelief, struggled to keep himself upright.

The bandit made a sound that was a combination cough and laugh, choking out, "I told you, Señor Kane: To teach a woman to shoot, that is a very bad thing." As Morales stumbled backward, the railing of the catwalk caught him behind his knees. He fell over the edge and landed with a thud on the ground below.

At the same time two shots were fired from Cull's room, and from the street beneath the window came loud cries and shouts, followed by the hoofbeats of a number of horses galloping out of town.

"They're gone!" Whisters called from Gideon Cull's window. "And they left their wagon in their hurry!"

From behind Kane, Loomis stepped into the room and asked, "You all right?"

Kane did not answer. Kneeling on the floor beside Crystal, he gently pried the gun from her fingers, which had seemingly frozen to the grip, then untied the gag from her mouth. He gazed for a moment at Crystal's face. When he was sure of his answer, he finally replied to Loomis's question. "We're all right," he said softly.

"I'm going down and check for more Mexicans—and to check out that wagon."

Kane nodded absently, still focused on Crystal's face as he untied the ropes binding her wrists, then her ankles. "It's over," he told her tenderly. "Crystal? Do you hear me? It's over."

Her eyes stared at the window. "I—I shot him," she mumbled in an almost inaudible voice. "I killed him." Her hands free now, Crystal covered her face with them and began to sob.

Her whole body trembled, and Kane held the young woman firmly by her shoulders. "Crystal! *Crystal!*"

She pulled back, then looked at him as if just aware of his presence. "Rado? Rado! You're safe!"

He smiled. "Thanks to you I am yes Are you all right?"

She looked back at the window, her eyes wide. "I just shot a man," she said with disbelief. Looking at Kane again, she returned his smile. "And, yes, I am all right."

Kane helped her to her feet and held her close to him. Her shaking began again, and he had to hold her tightly for several minutes before it stopped. When it did, he lifted her face, which was wet with tears.

"You were right about guns," she told him with a small smile.

"What about them?"

"It's not the guns that matter. It's who's on either end."

Five minutes later Rado Kane and Crystal Richmond joined the crowd below. The shots from the hotel had attracted most of the saloon crowd, and when the focus of attention had shifted to the rear of the building, the crowd had shifted there as well.

Standing beside the wagon were Sam Loomis and

Walt Grader, along with Katherine Mallory and David Garlath. The two young people were rubbing their wrists, which showed red welts where ropes had bound them tightly, and they were trying to get back the circulation that had been blocked by their restraints.

Nodding toward them, Loomis explained to Kane, "Another of Morales's ideas. He'd captured the two of them on their way back here—had them tied up in sacks, for God's sake!—and planned to hold the boy for ransom. As for the girl . . ."

"I know exactly what he had in mind," Crystal said, shuddering.

"Where *is* Morales?" Kane asked, looking around.

Loomis shook his head. "Don't know. He's not here, though. He must've rode off with his men."

Kane looked at Crystal, then back at the shotgun guard. "Last time we saw him, he didn't look to be in much shape to ride."

"Well, the fact is that dead or alive or somewhere in between, he ain't around here."

"Mr. Kane," Katherine Mallory spoke up, "we've heard about what you did. I can't believe you actually got our fathers to shoot at each other, but somehow you did it—and it was the right thing to do. Even if one of them might have killed the other."

Kane grinned crookedly. "There wasn't too much of a chance of that. I made sure they were standing a good distance away from each other—far enough so they'd have to be damned good with a gun to actually kill somebody." He threw a glance at David Garlath, then looked back at Katherine. "The biggest wounds they have are to their pride, but they'll get over it."

"They'd better," David said. "Katherine and I aren't waiting any longer. We're getting married as soon as possible, and we're going to talk our fathers into consolidating the two mines and operating them as one." He beamed with pleasure at Let Cutler and Clay Brock. "The foremen have agreed to help us and assure us the rest of the men will, too. We're going to work the mines until we know whether there's any real lode there or not. We should know soon whether we're financially all right or downright broke."

Isabel Hallan, her short white hair looking almost like a halo in the moonlight, stepped beside Katherine. "I believe I might be of some help, if you'd like." She then smiled at Crystal, adding, "I did mention to you that I might be delaying my going on to Tucson."

"Take her up on her offer," Crystal advised the young blonde. "I don't believe you'll be sorry."

"Of course," Mrs. Hallan said, winking at Crystal, "none of us can *know* that!"

Just then Whisters sidled up to Kane, saying softly, "Kane, could I have a word with you in private?"

As Kane followed the salesman around the corner of the building, he noticed that Whisters was gripping a familiar satchel—the one that had belonged to the Reverend Gideon Cull.

"The preacher's in his room, dead," Whisters explained. "No doubt killed by Morales or one of his men." He reached into the bag and handed a clasped Bible to Kane. "This is a very special book."

Kane unclasped the Bible and opened it. Most of the Word of the Lord had been cut out, leaving nothing but the outside page borders intact. Inside the neatly hollowed-out box was a stack of paper money and gold coins, plus golden earrings, pendants, and other jewelry made of pearls and what appeared to be precious stones.

"A *very* special book," Kane agreed.

"But not unique," Whisters informed him. "There are three others in here just like it. Also some plain old undoctored Bibles." The peddler studied the gunfighter for a long moment, then said, "The question is what to do with them."

Kane cocked his head slightly and peered at the salesman. "You could've kept them all for yourself."

Whisters's pudgy face broke into a smile. "Whatever

could I do with all this?" he quipped. "However, as a finder's fee, I do indeed intend to keep one. I've never had too much opportunity to build a retirement fund." Taking a book from the bag, he then handed the satchel to Kane. "As for the others, I'll leave that to you. I don't like to be involved."

Kane grinned. "For somebody who doesn't like to be involved, Mr. Whisters, you have an odd way of showing it." He extended his right hand. "Thanks. Not for this; for everything."

Whisters shook Kane's hand, then inquired, "There's one other thing. Is Miss Richmond still planning on going to Tucson?"

"I don't know," Kane replied quietly.

"Well, as I've said, I don't like to involve myself in others' business, but there is something I believe she should know."

When he had said what it was, Kane smiled. Looking down at the Bibles in the satchel, the gunfighter then asked, "Do these clasps lock?"

"I would imagine so," Whisters answered. "The keys are in the bag."

Kane found them and locked each of the leather clasps in place. Then he threw the keys under a squat cactus plant by the side of the building. "Shall we join the others?" he suggested.

When they reached the wagon, Kane presented one of the books to Katherine Mallory. "This is a wedding gift to the two of you from the Reverend Gideon Cull. Unfortunately he can't be with us this evening."

Whisters laughed. So did Loomis.

"Sam, this one's for you."

The shotgunner's grin changed to a look of surprise. "I've got no need for a Good Book, Kane," Loomis protested, shaking his head.

"This one you do," Whisters insisted. "Take it. And remember, all good things are better if they're shared. You may want to keep Walt in mind. He may have the same spiritual needs that you do."

Both Loomis and Grader looked bewildered as the shotgun guard took the proffered Bible. "It's locked," Loomis then remarked.

"So is this one," said Katherine.

"They all are," Kane informed them. "I don't know where the keys got to, but a little careful knife work will surely take care of it." He put the last Bible in Crystal Richmond's hands.

"What is this, Rado?" she asked with a nervous laugh. "Some kind of mass conversion?"

"Call it an act of providence," Kane retorted. "And you and I need to talk."

"Yes, we do," she agreed softly.

He led her back to the same place where he and Whisters had held their conversation.

"Rado," she began, "I want to say—"

"Not yet. First . . ." He looked over at Whisters and gestured for the peddler to join them. "Mr. Whisters, as you know, Miss Richmond here has plans to go on to Tucson. To work with a Miss—er—" He looked at Crystal.

"Annie Gantlin," she said, supplying the name.

"Mr. Whisters," Kane continued, "this Annie Gantlin. What was it you were telling me about her?"

"Simply that she owns a saloon and says she is establishing a theater, which attracts a lot of hopeful actresses, singers, and dancers. Simply that."

"And simply what else?" Kane prodded.

"Well, simply that the young women who are attracted to the theater mostly wind up in another of Annie's businesses." He shook his head ruefully. "I'm afraid, Miss Richmond, that your friend is the biggest madam in the whole Tucson area."

Crystal's eyes closed and she moaned. "There goes my new career. Gone before it started. Well, now what do I do?"

"There's always San Francisco again," the gunfighter suggested. "Or you can go back to Chicago."

The young woman looked at him with narrowed eyes.

"Or," he continued, "as you know, I've got a similar problem myself. I've got no job here or anywhere else, and I've been thinking a lot lately about what a man named Calvin Dunny once told me. The point is, I've been hearing about a line of work that, well, might be a little more peaceful than the one I've been in. With Loomis and Grader to put in a good word—"

"Do you mean it?" Crystal asked, her eyes widening.

"Excuse me," Whisters said quietly, tipping his bowler. "I really do need to be somewhere else. Don't know where that is, exactly, but it may as well be the saloon. There are sales to make—that's *my* work, you know. And bets to collect. And perhaps someone there might, after tonight's events, be interested in less violent entertainment"—he grinned—"like poker. I believe I'll ask Mrs. Hallan to join me. A temporary partnership might prove profitable to us both." With that he was gone.

Looking into Rado Kane's eyes, Crystal repeated her question. "Do you mean it? About being a stationmaster?"

"I mean it," Kane responded, standing as close to Crystal as was possible without their bodies actually touching. "Only thing is, I'd need a good woman. You know where I might find one?"

Her brow furrowed in thought, then she brightened. "You might try looking right here in Gila Bend."

They were suddenly in each other's arms. "Fortune smiles," Kane murmured, meeting her lips hungrily.

They finally broke apart. "It does?" she asked, catching her breath.

"Sure. I thought I might have to look as far away as Phoenix."

"Shut up," she said with a laugh. "Or—"

"Or?"

"Or I'll shoot—and this time I won't miss!"

STAGECOACH STATION 50:
BUCKSKIN PASS
by Hank Mitchum

Having hung up his gun two years ago, Clay Edwards looks forward to continuing his peaceful life as foreman of the Diamond J Ranch. But his calm existence is shattered when the murderous C. K. Moxley frames him for robbery and he is sentenced to ten years in the Colorado State Penitentiary.

Desperate to prove his innocence, Clay escapes prison and sets out to find Moxley, knowing the only chance of clearing himself lies in forcing the outlaw to tell the truth. Heading for Buckskin Pass high in the Rocky Mountains, where Moxley is holed up in a cabin, Clay joins a group of travelers riding the last stagecoach to cross the mountains before winter sets in. But the journey ends tragically when the stage is attacked by Indians, and all the passengers are killed except Clay and a beautiful young woman named Barbara LaBonde, who is on the run from her brutal, abusive husband.

Before Clay can hope to find Moxley and clear himself, he must overcome raging blizzards, fierce Utes, and severe injury. But his greatest challenge is to tear down the wall that the courageous Barbara has erected to ensure that no man will ever again get close enough to hurt her—not even one who has fallen deeply in love with her.

Read BUCKSKIN PASS, *on sale November 1990 wherever Bantam paperbacks are sold.*

★ WAGONS WEST ★

This continuing, magnificent saga recounts the adventures of a brave band of settlers, all of different backgrounds, all sharing one dream—to find a new and better life.

☐	26822	INDEPENDENCE! #1	$4.50
☐	26162	NEBRASKA! #2	$4.50
☐	26242	WYOMING! #3	$4.50
☐	26072	OREGON! #4	$4.50
☐	26070	TEXAS! #5	$4.50
☐	26377	CALIFORNIA! #6	$4.50
☐	26546	COLORADO! #7	$4.50
☐	26069	NEVADA! #8	$4.50
☐	26163	WASHINGTON! #9	$4.50
☐	26073	MONTANA! #10	$4.50
☐	26184	DAKOTA! #11	$4.50
☐	26521	UTAH! #12	$4.50
☐	26071	IDAHO! #13	$4.50
☐	26367	MISSOURI! #14	$4.50
☐	27141	MISSISSIPPI! #15	$4.50
☐	25247	LOUISIANA! #16	$4.50
☐	25622	TENNESSEE! #17	$4.50
☐	26022	ILLINOIS! #18	$4.50
☐	26533	WISCONSIN! #19	$4.50
☐	26849	KENTUCKY! #20	$4.50
☐	27065	ARIZONA! #21	$4.50
☐	27458	NEW MEXICO! #22	$4.50
☐	27703	OKLAHOMA! #23	$4.50
☐	28180	CELEBRATION! #24	$4.50